RAGS
TO RICHES

One

"So, how does it feel to turn into a millionaire's son overnight?" Olivia Davidson asked Roger Barrett. They were eating lunch together in the crowded cafeteria of Sweet Valley High, but neither was paying much attention to the food. Olivia pulled her brown, frizzy hair back from her face as she looked at Roger. Petite and pretty, Olivia was the arts editor of *The Oracle*, Sweet Valley High's newspaper, and her clothing was decidedly more Bohemian than that of most of her classmates. That day she was wearing an oversized cotton sweater belted with an Indian sash over a fringed skirt.

Roger shook his head. "I can't believe this is

the first time we've been alone since all this happened," he said. "I feel like I haven't had a minute to myself all week!"

"I know," Olivia said, putting her hand on Roger's arm and smiling sympathetically into his gray eyes. She couldn't believe it had been only a little over a week since Roger's mother had died of a heart attack and Henry Wilson Patman, one of the richest men in all of Sweet Valley, had announced Roger's real identity. This was Roger's first day back in school.

"It's all so strange," Roger told her. "One minute I'm Roger Barrett, a total nothing from a terrible family, and the next minute my mother's so sick, and Mr. Patman—uh, I mean, Uncle Henry—is sending her to Houston for an operation. And then she's dead. And as soon as the funeral's over, all these lawyers are swarming all over me, telling me I'm not Roger Barrett after all, but the son of Paul Patman." Roger looked down at the uneaten hot dog on his lunch tray and shook his head. "Liv, I don't know what to think about anything anymore," he confided.

Olivia tightened her hand on Roger's arm and was quiet for a minute. She was as dazed by the events of the last week as Roger. Her relationship with him had a long history. She had stuck by him when other people were making fun of him because they'd found out he was working as a janitor after school to help his mother pay the rent. Eventually, the two had come to love each other. *But being in love with Roger is like being on a*

2

roller coaster, she thought now. *First I had to help him realize that it didn't matter how poor his family was, that I didn't care about his background. And now suddenly he's a millionaire, living in the Patman mansion.*

Roger had even started to look different, Olivia thought. He was now wearing contact lenses, instead of his glasses, and he had on neat corduroys instead of his old jeans. Olivia couldn't even imagine what it would be like to move from the tiny place Roger had lived in with his mother into the Patmans' enormous mansion. What she *could* imagine was how lonesome Roger must be feeling now, cut off from everything he'd known before. "I just want you to know that I'm around if you need me," Olivia whispered. Roger smiled at her, and Olivia felt better. *He's still the same old Roger*, she thought to herself. *The Patmans may be terrible snobs, but they can't change him. No one can.*

"Roger, do you feel like telling me the story about your mother and—and Paul Patman?" Olivia asked. "All I know is what you told me the day your mother died. Since then, I've heard so many rumors that I'm not sure what the real story is."

"Well, according to Uncle Henry, this is the story. When my mother first moved to Sweet Valley, she took a job working for the Patmans. That was before Uncle Henry was married or had a family. He was living with his older brother, Paul, who was married to this woman everyone

3

hated. Well, I guess my mother fell in love with Paul Patman, and they spent more and more time together, and—" Roger stopped, his face turning red.

"I understand, Roger," Olivia said softly.

"Well, I guess my mother moved away when she found out she was going to have a baby. While she was gone, Paul tried to divorce his awful wife. He wanted to marry my mother. But nobody ever found out about it because he was killed in a plane crash flying down to Mexico on business."

"Oh, Roger, your poor mother," Olivia whispered.

"She never told me anything about it," Roger said. "No one did. Uncle Henry said that he tried to get her to take money at first, but she refused. What she didn't know was that Paul—my father—had left every nickel he had to me. He made a special provision in his will that I wasn't supposed to find out until I turned twenty-one, unless something happened to my mother."

"Why do you suppose he didn't want you to know?"

Roger shook his head. "I'm not exactly sure. I've been wondering about that myself. Maybe he was afraid my mother would be upset about it. You know how proud she was. Or maybe he thought it would be hard for me to learn the truth, since they weren't married. But you know, Olivia, the one thing I *don't* feel is embarrassed."

Olivia looked at him proudly.

"I mean it," Roger said. "I'm proud of my mother, and I know she always did what she thought was the right thing, no matter how hard it was. That's why—" His voice broke off, and he looked down at his tray again.

"That's why what?" Olivia prompted.

Roger shook his head. "I just feel a little confused, that's all," he said softly. "I wish I knew how she would want me to act now. I wish she could let me know somehow how to change overnight from Roger Barrett to Roger Patman."

Olivia stared at him uneasily. She loved Roger, and it almost broke her heart to think of his losing everything familiar to him in so short a time—his mother, his home, even his name. But she couldn't help but wonder, looking at the anxious expression on his familiar face, what place Roger Barrett's girlfriend would have in Roger Patman's new life.

Sweet Valley was buzzing with excitement over the news the Patmans' lawyers had disclosed after Roger's mother died. Who could ever have guessed that so much lay concealed behind the stately exterior of the Patman estate? Out of the blue, a poor orphan had been transformed into one of the richest young men in town—as rich as Bruce Patman, Henry Patman's son and now Roger's cousin. The students at Sweet Valley High had talked about nothing else for the past week. Questions and rumors were flying. Would Roger change, now that he was so rich? Did Bruce really resent him for moving into the Patman mansion? And was it true that Mrs. Patman couldn't bear the sight of her new nephew? While Olivia and Roger were eating lunch, they were being watched from all corners of the room.

"I think he looks as nerdy as ever," Lila Fowler told Jessica Wakefield as they watched Roger from across the cafeteria.

Jessica giggled. "You sure you're not just a little jealous, Lila?" she asked, following her friend's gaze.

Lila flushed. A while back Roger had had a wild crush on Lila and would have done anything to spend time with her. But Lila had been appalled when she found out how poor his family was. Her family was as wealthy as the Patmans, and she was used to dating boys who had cars and credit cards at their disposal—not boys who worked as janitors after school. But Lila had changed her mind about Roger when he won the Bart, the annual track competition. Overnight Roger had become a hero, and Lila had done her best to share his glory. But by then Olivia was already in the picture, and Lila was too late.

"Oh, come on, Jessica. All that was *ages* ago," Lila said. "I couldn't care less about Roger Barrett *or* Roger Patman. And I think he still looks pretty scruffy."

Jessica was only half listening to her friend.

6

She was looking anxiously around the cafeteria for her twin sister, Elizabeth, to ask for a ride home from cheerleading practice that afternoon.

Jessica and Elizabeth were identical twins, mirror images, even down to the dimple each had on her left cheek. They both had shoulder-length, sun-streaked blond hair, sparkling blue-green eyes, and perfect size-six figures. And they both wore matching gold lavalieres their parents had given them for their sixteenth birthday. Only people who knew the twins extremely well noticed that Elizabeth wore a watch, while Jessica never did. Jessica never cared about time—unless she wanted something in a hurry, as she did right then. "Where *is* that twin of mine?" she muttered. Jessica didn't like to be kept waiting—and as a rule, she didn't have to be.

"Jess, you're not even listening to me," Lila complained, tossing her wavy, shoulder-length brown hair back.

Jessica sighed, trying to listen to her friend. But she wasn't sure she agreed with Lila about Roger. She'd never really taken him seriously before, but Jessica thought he actually looked kind of cute right then, leaning his cheek on his hand and talking seriously to Olivia.

"Jessica, what in the world are you daydreaming about? I just asked you who you're going to the party with!" Lila exclaimed.

At the mention of the word "party," Jessica snapped out of her reverie. There was nothing Jessica loved as much as a party, and this wasn't just any party Lila was referring to. It promised to be just about the biggest social event of the season, if not the whole year. The Patmans had decided to welcome their new nephew by giving a formal dance at the Sweet Valley Country Club, the most exclusive club for miles around.

"I haven't decided yet," Jessica said. As she spoke, she saw Olivia put her hand on Roger's arm, and a strange shiver passed through her. For a long time Jessica had been enchanted by the Patmans. She had wished that her own family lived in one of the huge mansions up on the hill overlooking Sweet Valley. As a matter of fact, Bruce Patman was one of the few boys Jessica had ever really fallen for. That had ended ages ago, and now Jessica could barely stand the sight of Bruce. But it occurred to her that there might be another Patman around who was a little more interesting. *I wonder*, Jessica thought, giving Roger and Olivia a good long look, *what it would be like to go to the dance with the guest of honor himself—the richest young man in Sweet Valley.*

"Haven't decided what?" a high-pitched voice demanded. Jessica and Lila looked up into the eager face of Caroline Pearce, a girl who had long ago forged herself the reputation as the biggest gossip in the school.

"Nothing, Caroline," Lila said firmly, standing up and picking up her tray to discourage Caroline from pumping her further. "I'll call you tonight, Jess," Lila said, walking away. A second later Jessica bounced out of her chair, Roger

Patman and the country club dance temporarily forgotten in the excitement of finally spotting her twin on the other side of the room. Curious, Caroline Pearce stared after her.

"Liz, *wait!*" Jessica hollered, catching her sister just as she was heading out to the corridor with Todd Wilkins, her steady boyfriend.

"I get the impression that Jessica needs you for some reason," Todd said dryly, his brown eyes sparkling with amusement.

"Liz, can you give me a ride home after cheerleading? Neil couldn't get the car today, and I absolutely swore to Mom that I'd clean my room before dinner."

Elizabeth groaned. "We'd better leave now, if you really intend to let anyone even past your door by dinner," she told her sister. Jessica's room was an old joke in the Wakefield family. She had insisted on painting her walls chocolate brown, which had earned it its nickname "The Hershey Bar." And it was almost always impossible to get much past Jessica's door—usually because the entire contents of her closet were strewn all over the floor.

"OK," Elizabeth conceded, laughing at the pleading expression on her twin's face. Elizabeth could rarely hold out on Jessica. "I'm working late at the *Oracle* office, and I'll meet you when I'm done." Elizabeth wrote "Eyes and Ears," the gossip column for the school newspaper. She hoped the job might help her to realize her dream of becoming a writer.

Elizabeth and Todd watched Jessica bound away, and Todd laughed. "It's a good thing I've got the sane half of this package," he teased Elizabeth, kissing the tip of her nose.

Elizabeth smiled up at him. "Walk me to class?" she asked.

"Hey, Miss Eyes and Ears," Todd said as they walked down the hall toward Elizabeth's English class, "what do you think of all this business about Roger Barrett Patman?"

"I'm not sure," Elizabeth said, growing serious. "You know I've always liked Roger. I felt so sorry for him when his mother was sick, and I guess my first feeling when I heard the news was relief that he'd have a family to go to now. But—"

"But you have your doubts about the family he's gone to," Todd finished for her.

Elizabeth sighed. "It's not my business, really," she said. "I just hope he'll be all right. There must be a lot of pressure on him, and he's already been through so much."

Todd nodded. "One more question," he said.

"What now?" she asked. Elizabeth stopped walking and looked up at Todd quizzically.

"I just wondered," Todd said, "if you'd noticed anything else going on around here that's a little out of the ordinary."

"What do you mean?"

"Have you noticed anything odd lately about Regina Morrow?"

Regina Morrow was a new girl at Sweet Valley

High. During her first few weeks at school, an aura of mystery had surrounded her—in part, because she was fabulously wealthy and beautiful, with long, dark hair and high cheekbones; and in part because Regina was almost completely deaf. She had refused to be given special treatment because of her handicap. She had studied lipreading for years at a school in Boston and was able to keep up with all her classes at Sweet Valley—in fact, able to do honors work in most of her subjects. Before long, many of her classmates had almost forgotten that she was deaf. But no one had forgotten that Regina was beautiful.

"Todd, what are you talking about?" Elizabeth demanded, her reporter's curiosity getting the better of her.

"Time for study hall," Todd said, grinning as he walked away. "I'll talk to you tonight," he called to her, his voice maddeningly mysterious.

Elizabeth stared after him, her brow wrinkled. What in the world could be going on with Regina Morrow? She couldn't believe Todd had just left her in midair this way—and now she had a whole English class to sit through! Oh, well, it looked as if she was just going to have to be patient until that night.

Two

The Patman mansion was nestled high on a hill in Sweet Valley, set back from the road that curved up around the most expensive real estate in the area. "Home sweet home, little cousin," Bruce Patman said sarcastically, expertly maneuvering his black Porsche up the steep driveway to the Patmans' five-car garage. Roger swallowed nervously. He wondered how long it would take before he felt comfortable in this enormous estate. Bruce wasn't making things easier, either. Bruce had never been very nice to Roger; and ever since Roger had run against Bruce in the Bart and won, they had not been on good terms. Bruce slammed the door shut on the

12

driver's side of the car and raced to the side entrance of the house. "Come on," he yelled behind him. "We've got guests for dinner, remember?"

Roger followed slowly behind his new cousin. He *did* remember. In fact, all day he had thought about little else. The previous evening Mrs. Patman had called him into her bedroom. She was sitting in front of her vanity mirror, smoothing beauty cream into the skin around her eyes. "Roger," she'd said coolly, her eyes fixed on the mirror, "we have some important guests coming to dinner tomorrow night. Their name is Ferguson, and Mr. Ferguson is a special client of Mr. Patman's. It's very important," she had added, "that you make a good impression on them."

Roger remembered just standing there, feeling clumsy and embarrassed. Ever since he'd moved in with the Patmans, his new aunt had been lecturing him about making a good impression. It seemed that nothing he did was right. He wore the wrong clothes; he talked about the wrong things; he treated the servants as friends instead of hired help.

"What are those things you've got on your feet, dear?" Mrs. Patman had suddenly asked him, turning her cold blue eyes downward with a look of disdain.

Roger had looked down at his old running shoes and back up at his aunt. "Uh, nothing," he'd answered, turning bright red. "Just what I usually wear," he'd added quickly.

"I see," Mrs. Patman had said archly. "I thought your uncle had done something about your clothes already. Well, we'll have to make sure to get rid of those things and buy you some decent shoes," she'd added, looking back in the mirror and putting more cream on her throat. "In the meantime, dear, maybe you'd better let Bruce help you find something suitable for dinner tomorrow evening. Bruce is so clever with clothes. And"—she had swiveled around in her chair for emphasis, giving Roger one last penetrating stare—"we *do* want to please the Fergusons."

"Yes, ma'am," Roger had muttered, staring down at the thick, cream-colored carpeting.

"Just remember," she'd called after him as he'd stumbled toward the bedroom door, "keep an eye on Bruce if you're uncertain about anything. He always knows what to do. I'm sure you'll be a splendid success. After all, we're counting on you to keep up the Patman name."

Now, as Roger walked up the imposing staircase inside the Patman home and closed the door to his new bedroom behind him, he wondered if he'd ever fit in with the Patmans. He still couldn't get over this room. His bedroom at home hadn't been as big as his dressing room here. And this bedroom was almost half as big as his old house! An enormous four-poster bed stood in the middle of the room. In one corner, a mahogany writing desk stood beneath shelf after shelf of leather-bound books. Roger had never even heard of half the titles. The room was deafeningly quiet. And despite its grandeur, there was nothing in it that he used to long for when he was poor—no stereo, no games, no sports equipment. Small as it had been, Roger's old room had felt a lot more like home than this place.

Roger opened the door to his dressing room and tried to decide what to wear to dinner. He felt all thumbs, putting on the new clothes his uncle had just bought him. He had to tie his tie five times before it looked right, and it still seemed to be choking him. And no matter how much water he put on his hair, one funny little tuft kept sticking straight up on top. Roger walked to the full-length mirror at the end of his dressing room and examined himself from all angles. He looked like a stranger—creased chino trousers, a navy blazer, silk striped tie, and a starched cotton shirt.

Someone was knocking on his bedroom door, and before Roger could say anything, the door swung open, and Bruce, looking immaculate and perfectly at ease, strolled over to the dressing room. "Hope you're ready for old Fergie, Rog," he said cheerfully, leaning against the door frame. "He can be a real terror."

Roger swallowed hard. He had the feeling that he'd be better off staying up in his room all evening.

"Well, well, well," Bruce said, coming closer to Roger. "Don't we look spiffy tonight! Not the Roger we used to know, that's for sure."

Roger flushed. "Take it easy, Bruce," he said, fighting to keep his voice calm. "I feel even stranger than I look."

Bruce snorted. "That would be hard," he muttered.

Roger followed Bruce down to the main dining room, where dinner was to be served. *It's funny,* he thought, *but it's almost a relief to be around Bruce. At least he comes right out in the open and acts like he hates me.* Mrs. Patman was a lot more subtle, and every time she called him "dear" he could feel himself wincing.

Roger almost burst out laughing when he saw the six place settings laid out on the sprawling table. Thirty people could have fit around the table with ease, and with only six plates it seemed as if there was a mile of polished wood between each person.

But Roger didn't feel like laughing anymore when Mrs. Patman fixed her icy gaze on him. "You remember Bruce," she told the two guests, who were standing between her and Mr. Patman. "And this, of course, is Roger."

Roger looked from one Ferguson to the other. Mr. Ferguson was in his late sixties. His white hair was brushed back, and he had a distinguished, suntanned face. His eyes were small and black, and he looked at Roger as if the boy were a stray dog at an animal shelter. "Oh, yes, I see," he said, nodding his head several times in rapid succession. Mrs. Ferguson was much younger than her husband. Roger stared at her hands. He had never in his whole life seen diamonds so big—nor, for that matter, nails so long.

"Pleased to meet you, boy," Mr. Ferguson said, thrusting his hand out. Roger shook it uneasily.

"Delighted, I'm sure," Mrs. Ferguson said, looking straight past Roger and sounding bored out of her mind. Roger reached out to shake her hand, too, and she looked down at it with amused disdain. Roger thrust his hand back in his pocket. *Strike one*, he thought to himself.

"Roger, why don't you sit over here, dear," Mrs. Patman said. Mr. Patman sat at the head of the table, and Mrs. Patman sat down at the other end. Roger sat across from Bruce, with Mrs. Ferguson at his left. *Good Lord*, he thought to himself, looking down at the place setting in front of him. He had never seen so much silverware. He counted under his breath, four—no five—separate forks! What on earth was he supposed to do with them?

Reginald, the Patmans' waiter, brought a silver decanter into the dining room and poured wine while Miranda brought salad from the kitchen. *So far so good*, thought Roger. No one seemed to be paying attention to him, and it looked as though he might just get through this ordeal without disaster.

"I still can't believe you bought that stock

when I told you to sell," Mr. Ferguson said to Mr. Patman, launching into a business conversation.

Mrs. Ferguson ignored Roger and fixed her gaze on Bruce. "What about you, dear?" she asked sternly. "Have you been involving yourself a little more in the art world these days?"

"Uh—not as much as I should be," Bruce said, smiling at her with sickening insincerity.

Roger tried to keep a straight face. Bruce involving himself with the arts? *I wonder if she's talking about taking girls to drive-in movies*, he thought. *Only Bruce never sees more than the first ten minutes of those.*

Miranda placed a salad plate in front of him, and Roger studied it carefully and counted the forks again under his breath. *It must be this one*, he told himself, picking up the fork closest to his plate.

"The other one, Rog," Bruce told him, helpful now that he had an audience. "The one on the outside."

Roger turned beet red. *Strike two*, he thought, hastily putting the fork down and picking up the one farthest to his left and closest to Mrs. Ferguson, who was staring at him with a mixture of fascination and horror.

"Do you think," she asked him, her voice going all funny and high-pitched, "that I might possibly have the bread basket?"

"Sure thing," Roger said. He reached out for the basket, and as he passed it to Mrs. Ferguson, the sleeve of his blazer caught on his full glass of red wine, which spilled all over the white tablecloth. Drops of wine spattered in Mrs. Ferguson's direction.

"My word," Mr. Ferguson said loudly, jumping out of his chair. "Are you all right, Marjorie?"

"Roger, how careless of you," Mrs. Patman said acidly.

"It's nothing, only a little wine," Mr. Patman boomed cheerfully, ringing the small bell at his right to call Miranda in from the kitchen.

"It's positively *ruined* my dress," Mrs. Ferguson told her husband, scrubbing furiously at the microscopic fleck of red that had splashed on her dress.

Roger stared down at the spreading stain of ruby-colored wine, his face flaming to the roots of his hair. "I—uh—will you excuse me, please," he stammered, jumping up from his chair, and before anyone could say another word, he shot out of the room and raced to the grand staircase. He could hear Mrs. Patman apologizing for his behavior, but he didn't care. He just wanted to be alone, away from the Patmans and the Fergusons and the servants and the dozens of forks. Roger raced upstairs and slammed his bedroom door behind him. He ran over to the huge bay window overlooking the rolling grass of the Patman estate and pressed his burning forehead against the glass. In all his life he had never felt so confused, and so terribly alone.

*　　*　　*

"Do you have to do that in here?" Elizabeth demanded. Jessica was stretched out on the floor in Elizabeth's cream-colored bedroom, doing Jane Fonda exercises to the tape in her Walkman.

"What?" Jessica asked, taking her headphones off.

"It's not that I don't like your company," Elizabeth said dryly, "but I'm expecting a phone call from Todd."

The Wakefield twins were upstairs in their comfortable split-level house, relaxing by themselves after dinner.

"But there isn't a single square inch of space in my room, Liz," Jessica grumbled.

"I thought you were supposed to clean it this afternoon," Elizabeth reminded her.

"I know, but I'm painting T-shirts for the cheerleaders' garage sale, and they're all hanging up to dry now," Jessica explained. "Let me just stay until Todd calls," she begged her twin.

"All right," Elizabeth agreed.

Jessica took her earphones off and started lifting her long, shapely legs. "Elizabeth," she began, talking between lifts, "don't you think Roger looks different these days?"

"He looks the same to me," Elizabeth answered.

"I think he's kind of cute," Jessica went on.

"I guess so." Elizabeth stared at the phone.

"What are you going to wear to the Patmans' party?" Jessica asked.

20

"I don't know yet," Elizabeth said. What could be keeping Todd? All afternoon she'd been wondering what he'd meant about Regina Morrow.

"I suppose Roger will take Olivia to the party," Jessica continued, abandoning her leg lifts and holding her legs straight out before her so she could admire them.

"I suppose so," Elizabeth agreed.

Jessica scrambled up from the floor and went to the mirror over her twin's dresser, picking up a hairbrush and running it through her long, blond hair. "I think my face is getting rounder," she said critically.

"Your face is the same shape it's always been, Jess," Elizabeth said, laughing. "And the same shape mine is. So leave it alone!"

"Maybe I'll buy a new dress for the party," Jessica said. "Something really *elegant*." Already she was beginning to devise a plan. She pictured herself in a soft, full-length dress, dancing slowly in the arms of Roger Patman while the rest of the guests looked on and clapped. *Olivia Davidson*, she thought to herself, *is hardly the right sort of girl to go out with Roger Patman. She may have been fine for Roger Barrett, but Roger Patman needs someone a little more exciting.* Jessica grinned at her reflection in the mirror. She had a pretty good idea of who that more exciting girl might be.

The phone rang, and Elizabeth dived for it, turning to her twin with a look as firm as it was fond.

"Back to the T-shirts!" Jessica sang cheerfully, scooping up her Walkman and banging the door closed behind her.

"Where have you been, Todd?" Elizabeth said into the phone. "How dare you leave me here dying with curiosity all night!"

Todd chuckled. "Sorry, but I was down at the repair shop. It looks like it'll be another week before they can get the part I need for the old Datsun." Todd's car had broken down on the way to Elizabeth's house the previous week.

"OK, so tell me what you meant this afternoon," Elizabeth prompted, settling into her favorite chair and tucking her long legs underneath her.

"Liz, I'm worried about Regina," Todd said. "Haven't you noticed anything strange about the way she's been acting?"

"What do you mean by 'strange'?" Elizabeth asked, her curiosity aroused.

"Well, for one thing, she's been leaving school early. She's in my English class, which meets last period, and yesterday was the third time in the last two weeks she wasn't there. I see her at lunchtime, but by the end of the day she's gone. And yesterday after gym I saw her standing out in the parking lot, looking really nervous. I started to walk over to her, and when she saw me, she hurried away."

"Where did she go?" Elizabeth asked.

"That's what I'm not sure of," Todd told her. "I chased after her and asked her what was

22

wrong, and she turned bright red and hurried off as if she hadn't read my lips."

"That's strange," Elizabeth commented. "I wonder where she could be going?"

"And the other thing," Todd went on, "is that she's been acting real weird lately. She seems to be spending more and more time by herself."

"That's right!" Elizabeth exclaimed. "I saw her eating lunch alone today. What do you think is going on?"

"I don't know," Todd said. "But I have an idea how we can find out. Can you get the car tomorrow?"

"I don't know," Elizabeth said, wrinkling her brow. "My mom may need it, but I'll ask. Why, Todd?"

"If you can get the car," Todd told her, "I'll tell you my plan tomorrow."

Three

For once, Jessica was at the breakfast table before Elizabeth. "To what do I owe this unexpected pleasure?" Mr. Wakefield teased the younger of his twin daughters, putting aside the business section of the morning newspaper. With his wavy, dark hair, broad shoulders, and rugged good looks, the twins' father looked like an older version of their brother, Steven, who attended a college in the area. Ned Wakefield was a lawyer in Sweet Valley and was often at the office in the morning before the twins came downstairs.

"I'm getting a ride to school," Jessica told her father cheerfully, buttering an English muffin.

"Jess, would you mind telling me what that is

24

you're wearing?" Alice Wakefield asked, pouring her daughter a glass of orange juice. When their mother was around, it was easy to see where the Wakefield twins got their good looks. Petite, blond-haired, and blue-eyed, Alice Wakefield was sometimes mistaken for the twins' older sister.

"It's my latest idea for raising money for the cheerleaders," Jessica told her proudly, flipping her blond hair behind one shoulder and swiveling in her chair to show her parents the bold lines of colored paint she had splashed on a white T-shirt. "We're going to sell these and make a fortune!" Privately Jessica wasn't all that sure the T-shirts would be a financial success. But she knew the T-shirt she was wearing showed her tanned arms to their best advantage, and she had carefully chosen dabs of blue-green paint to match her sparkling eyes.

"Morning, Mom. Morning, Dad," Elizabeth said, giving her mother a quick hug and plopping down across from her twin. Pouring herself a big bowl of cereal, Elizabeth asked, "Mom, can I take the car again today?"

"I guess so," Mrs. Wakefield answered. "I can get a ride with your dad today." Alice Wakefield worked as an interior designer downtown. "Give your sister a ride if she needs one," she called over her shoulder, hurrying upstairs to finish dressing.

"I told you I'm getting a ride," Jessica shouted to her mother. "With Neil."

"Neil Freemount again?" Mr. Wakefield said teasingly. "Is the list of admirers narrowing down?"

Neil Freemount, as it happened, was one of the best-looking guys in the twins' class at Sweet Valley High. Good at sports, easy to get along with, and the proud owner of a brand-new sports car, Neil was very much in demand. Between boyfriends, Jessica didn't mind spending time with Neil, especially now that he had a car. "He's OK until something better comes along" was how Jessica described Neil to her best friend, Cara Walker. To her father she said airily, "Neil's just a friend, that's all. No one special."

"Oh, no!" Elizabeth exclaimed, looking at her watch. "I'm supposed to drop something off at the *Oracle* office before homeroom." She jumped up from the table, giving her father a quick kiss, waving at Jessica, and grabbing her books from the kitchen counter as she hurried toward the garage.

"Drive safely," her father called after her, and Elizabeth nodded, her blond ponytail bouncing.

I really shouldn't have asked for the car again today, Elizabeth thought, backing the small red Fiat Spider out of the garage and turning down the drive. She usually preferred to save the car for occasions when she couldn't get by without it. *What does Todd have in mind for this afternoon?* she wondered.

She drove slowly, enjoying the warm sunshine streaming through the open top of the car. For what must have been the millionth time, Elizabeth thought how lucky she was to live in Sweet Valley. She couldn't imagine a more beautiful town, she thought, catching a glimpse of green lawns and bright flower beds in her rearview window.

As she was driving, Elizabeth noticed a girl up ahead walking slowly, her arms filled with books. It was Olivia Davidson. Slowing the car to a full stop beside the girl, Elizabeth called, "Olivia! Can I give you a ride?"

Olivia grinned at her, pushing her frizzy hair behind her ear with a quick, nervous gesture. "That would be great, Liz," she replied, opening the door and climbing into the passenger's seat. "I'm late as it is, and I've got tons of stuff to get through for *The Oracle*. You'd think one day someone would send me something wonderful to read," she grumbled, laughing.

As arts editor for *The Oracle*, Olivia was always trying to sneak a few minutes between classes to read the poems and stories people submitted to be published. It occurred to Elizabeth that she hadn't seen Olivia around the *Oracle* office much lately. *Maybe that has something to do with what's happening with Roger*, Elizabeth thought. Elizabeth had always liked Olivia. As usual, she and Jessica were in complete disagreement in their choice of friends. Jessica thought Olivia was weird. "She's always dragging those drawings and poems around with her, and she wears such freaky clothes," was Jessica's usual observation.

But Elizabeth thought Olivia had a refreshing, natural beauty. She wore hardly any makeup, and she kept her curly, brown hair loose and simple. She was very slender and small, and what Jessica called "freaky" clothes suited her very well—Indian cotton wraparound skirts and simple V-necked T-shirts. Olivia looked especially pretty that day, Elizabeth thought. She was wearing a simple necklace made of rawhide and beads, and long silver earrings that made her look like a Mexican princess.

"What beautiful earrings!" Elizabeth exclaimed, starting the car again.

Olivia smiled. "Roger gave them to me for my birthday."

Elizabeth looked at her thoughtfully. "How's Roger doing, Olivia?" she asked. "Have all the sudden changes been hard on him?"

"I think they have, a little," Olivia said slowly. "It's funny. Most people wouldn't think it would be hard to turn into a millionaire overnight. But—" She paused, and Elizabeth thought she detected uneasiness on Olivia's lovely face. Olivia didn't finish her sentence, and Elizabeth decided not to press her.

"Are you looking forward to the barbecue at the Patmans' this Saturday?" she asked instead.

"Oh, yes," Olivia said quickly. *Almost too quickly*, Elizabeth thought.

The Patmans had decided to have an informal

party to welcome their new nephew before the big event at the country club, and Todd and the twins had been invited. "I've never been up to the Patmans' house before," Olivia continued, nervously twisting the rawhide bracelet on her slender wrist. "I think it's going to be fun."

"I think so, too," Elizabeth said gently. "You know, Olivia," she added, "I think Roger is really lucky to have a girlfriend like you. He probably needs you now more than ever.

Olivia didn't answer, but her smile told Elizabeth that she had said the right thing.

"Well, here we are!" Elizabeth exclaimed, pulling the car into the parking lot adjacent to Sweet Valley High. She glanced quickly at her watch as she turned the engine off. She had exactly five minutes until homeroom.

"Todd, I just don't feel right about this!" Elizabeth protested. Since lunchtime she had been anxious about Todd's plan, and now, sitting in the parking lot with Todd beside her in the passenger seat, she felt downright guilty.

"Come on, Liz," Todd cajoled. "We're only missing one class. And besides, what if Regina's in some kind of trouble?"

"I don't see how—" Elizabeth began, but Todd cut her off, putting his hand on her arm.

"There she is!" Todd cried. "OK, Liz, let's go!"

Regina Morrow had come out of the side door of Sweet Valley High. She glanced anxiously at

29

her watch and then all around her to make sure no one was looking. Then she darted across the parking lot.

"Wait until she's in front of us, and we'll follow her," Todd instructed.

"All right," Elizabeth agreed uneasily. Regina had crossed the parking lot now and was hurrying down the road that led away from the high school to the business district of Sweet Valley.

"Let's go," Todd urged.

Elizabeth drove as slowly as she could, keeping a close eye on Regina. "She really looks like she's in a hurry," she said. "How many times did you say you've seen her leave school early?"

"This is the fourth time in the last two weeks. Hey, Liz, watch that bus!"

Regina was boarding a downtown bus, and Elizabeth speeded up and moved the little red Fiat into the lane next to the bus.

"We've got to make this light!" Todd cried as the bus crossed the intersection in front of them.

"Todd, we are *not* going to get ourselves killed," Elizabeth said reproachfully, slowing down as the light in front of them turned from yellow to red.

"We've lost her now," Todd said, slumping in the front seat. Seeing the look on Elizabeth's face, he quickly changed his expression. "Sorry, Liz," he murmured. "I'm getting too involved in all this detective stuff. We'll catch up with that old bus."

It didn't take long to catch up to the bus, and at

each bus stop Elizabeth pulled up behind the bus and waited. When the bus reached the center of Sweet Valley High's business district, Regina got off.

Todd spotted Regina first. "There she is!" he cried. "Find a parking place—quick!"

Elizabeth pulled the car into a parking spot in front of the Sweet Valley Medical Center and then turned to look for Regina. She had crossed the street from the bus stop and was standing in front of a tall, mirrored building. She checked her watch, looked in both directions, and took a compact out of her bag.

"What's she doing?" Todd asked, his eyes fixed on Regina.

"Putting lipstick on," Elizabeth whispered. A few minutes later a tall, handsome man who appeared to be in his late thirties came up to Regina. He kissed her on the cheek, and Regina smiled up at him and told him something. The man took her arm. Regina looked around her nervously, and the two of them disappeared into the glamorous building, the glass doors closing behind them.

"What in the world do you think is going on?" Todd asked.

Elizabeth shook her head, but before she could answer, a high feminine voice interrupted them.

"Liz! Todd!" the voice squealed.

Elizabeth started guiltily and spun around to see Lila Fowler waving at them from the curb. "Well, isn't this a small world," Lila said gaily.

31

Elizabeth thought Lila was staring past them to the spot across the street where Regina had been standing, but she couldn't be sure. "I just had a dentist appointment," Lila said, grimacing. "What a way to spend a gorgeous afternoon! What brings you two downtown so early?" she went on, looking curiously from Todd to Elizabeth.

"We're meeting my father," Elizabeth said, surprised at how quickly the white lie slipped out. "His office is just around the corner."

"That's nice," Lila said breezily. "Well, I guess I'd better run. I've got to pick my dress up from the seamstress. You should see it, Liz. It's absolutely perfect for the Patmans' party. What are you going to wear?"

"I'm not sure yet," Elizabeth told her.

"Hey," Lila interrupted, squinting in the bright sunlight, "isn't that Roger now, over in front of The Sports Shop with Mr. Patman?"

"It sure is," Todd replied.

Lila gave Elizabeth a knowing smile. "It looks like *everybody* is downtown this afternoon," she said slyly.

"Now," Mr. Patman said, putting an arm around Roger, "I think it's high time we got you some decent running clothes."

Roger grinned at his new uncle. This was like a dream come true, he thought. For as long as he could remember, Roger had walked past The

Sports Shop on his way to work, staring at the running shoes in the window. It would have taken him months to save up enough for a pair of shoes like that, he thought, since all his money had gone for household expenses. It was hard to believe that now, with the help of the plastic credit card his uncle had given him, he could buy whatever he wanted without even looking at price tags.

"Let's start with a really good pair of shoes," Mr. Patman suggested, holding open the door to the shop. "And then a few pair of nylon shorts. OK?"

Before they had been in the store more than a few minutes, Roger's eye fell on an aluminum tennis racket in a display case. "Not bad," Mr. Patman said, examining it. "We'll take that racket, too," he told the salesman.

"Uncle Henry!" Roger protested. "I don't need my own tennis racket!"

Mr. Patman grinned at him. "You're forgetting something, Roger," he teased him. "You have your own courts now. What are you going to do without a racket?"

Forty minutes later, his arms laden with packages, Roger followed his uncle out to the car. "I don't know how to thank you for all this," he said.

Mr. Patman laughed. "Then don't!" he boomed cheerfully. "Just have a good time, Roger. That's all I ask."

Roger shook his head, getting into the back

seat of his uncle's limousine. As they drove in the direction of the Patman estate, Roger leaned back against the seat, a smile playing about his lips. He had forgotten about Bruce and Mrs. Patman and the Fergusons and the humiliation of the dinner party the night before. For now, all Roger remembered was that he was a Patman. And being a Patman suddenly looked like a pretty good thing.

Four

Saturday, the day of the Patmans' barbecue, proved to be absolutely beautiful. The sun was steady and bright in a cloudless sky, and the radio promised the temperature would rise to eighty degrees by midafternoon. "Perfect swimming weather!" Jessica exclaimed, holding up a brand-new bathing suit. "Wait until Roger sees this," she murmured to herself, slipping the sleek black maillot into her bag. Jessica usually preferred bikinis, thinking it was a shame to conceal her trim, tanned abdomen. But the salesgirl at Foxy Mama had convinced her that the maillot was much more sophisticated.

What I need, Jessica told herself, *is to get Roger's*

attention. Once he takes a good look at me, he'll realize that Olivia is completely wrong for him. And if I can get Roger to fall in love with me in the next two weeks, I'll be the date of the guest of honor at the biggest party of the whole season!

"Jess, Todd's been waiting downstairs for almost ten minutes," Elizabeth complained, sticking her head around Jessica's half-closed door. Elizabeth gasped. "What in the world is going on in here?" It looked as if Jessica had emptied the contents of her dresser drawers and closet onto her bed. Clothes were strewn everywhere. The only tidy thing in the entire room was Jessica herself, who looked absolutely stunning in a pair of crisp white tennis shorts and a turquoise polo shirt. A warning bell went off in Elizabeth's head. The last time she'd seen her twin dressed so conservatively was when she'd fallen madly in love with Bruce Patman and started buying clothes from The Boston Shop to please him.

"What's with the preppy look?" she demanded suspiciously.

Jessica shrugged, stepping over the piles of clothes on her floor to get to her dresser. "Just trying to look tidy, Liz," she said innocently, brushing her thick, sun-streaked blond hair until it shone. "Hey, Liz, is Regina coming this afternoon?"

Elizabeth's brow wrinkled. "I think so. At least, she said she was the last time I saw her.

Why?" Elizabeth demanded, looking closely at Jessica.

"Just wondering," Jessica said airily. Putting the hairbrush down, she turned from the mirror. "Maybe she'll bring that mysterious older man of hers," she said sweetly.

"Jessica Wakefield, what on earth are you talking about?"

Jessica shrugged. "Personally, I don't see what the big deal is," she said archly. "What's wrong with older men? Unless—"

"Unless?" Elizabeth prompted.

Jessica shook her head. "Well, you know, Liz, if he's really as old as everyone *says* he is, Regina could be getting herself into real trouble. You know how it is with older men," she concluded vaguely.

"Just who is this 'everyone' who told you that Regina is seeing an older man?" Elizabeth asked, her voice rising.

"Girls!" Mrs. Wakefield called upstairs, interrupting the twins' conversation. "Todd's been sitting down here for ages. What in the world is taking you so long?"

"Come on, Liz," Jessica said, grabbing her bag. She shook her head at her twin's irritated expression. "Liz, I couldn't care less *who* Regina Morrow goes out with," she insisted. "I'm just a little worried about her reputation, that's all."

There was an anxious expression on Elizabeth's pretty face as she followed her twin downstairs. She had a pretty good idea that the "everyone" who had told Jessica about Regina's companion was Lila Fowler. But why would Lila want to spread such vicious rumors about Regina?

The barbecue was being held out by the Patmans' Olympic-sized swimming pool. Tables had been set up under yellow-and-white umbrellas, where lunch would be served later on. By the time Todd and the twins arrived, the party was in full swing. Roger greeted them as they walked across the lawn. "Come say hello to my aunt and uncle," he urged them.

Todd shook hands with Mr. Patman while Elizabeth exchanged pleasantries with Roger's aunt. To Elizabeth's amazement, Jessica actually lingered behind to tell Mrs. Patman how pleased she was to have been invited. "I *love* your outfit," Jessica cooed. Personally Elizabeth thought that Mrs. Patman was overdressed for the occasion. Her long, silky, black hair looked a little too perfect to be her natural color, and the pink satin lounging pajamas she was wearing would have looked more appropriate on a Hollywood set. "And look at your beautiful flower beds!" Elizabeth heard her sister exclaim.

"Something is definitely going on with that girl today," Elizabeth murmured to Todd as they headed toward the pool.

"Liz! Todd! Over here!" Enid Rollins called, waving from the side of the pool. Her boyfriend,

George Warren, was sitting next to her. Elizabeth's face lit up. Aside from Todd, Enid was her very dearest friend. Jessica couldn't understand what Elizabeth saw in Enid, but Elizabeth knew that beneath Enid's shy exterior was a heart of gold. Todd and Elizabeth joined them by the deep end.

"This is really an incredible place, isn't it?" Enid said. Elizabeth nodded, looking around her. She recognized dozens of faces from school—Cara Walker, one of Jessica's best friends, talking to Bill Chase, the best surfer at Sweet Valley High; Neil Freemount, who had watched Elizabeth and Todd attentively as they approached, probably looking for Jessica; and Caroline Pearce, who was talking anxiously to Lila Fowler. Lila looked bored to death—her usual expression, Elizabeth thought—lying flat on her back in a lounge chair.

"Look, there's Regina!" Elizabeth exclaimed, nudging Todd. "And the only older man she's with is her brother Nicholas!" she said, giggling.

"I see Bruce has invited his usual assortment of older women," Enid noted.

Elizabeth laughed, following Enid's gaze. Bruce was standing and talking to several girls who appeared to be a couple of years older than Elizabeth. "Typical Bruce," she said, grinning. "I don't know where he finds them."

"I want to know where he found that bathing suit," George announced. "It's the tiniest thing I've ever seen."

"It looks like a Band-Aid," Todd agreed, laughing. "Hey, what's Olivia doing over there all by herself?" he asked, craning his neck.

Elizabeth turned around and followed his gaze. Olivia *was* sitting alone, and she looked distinctly uncomfortable. She was wearing a gauze sun dress, and from the way she was fingering the beads around her neck, Elizabeth guessed that she was nervous.

"Stay here for a minute," she told Todd. "I'm going to talk to her." She walked over to where Olivia was sitting.

"Hey, Liz!" Olivia said, brushing her curly hair back from her face. "You look great," she added.

"So do you, Olivia," Elizabeth said firmly. She wished Olivia would feel more confident about herself. "Where's Roger?" she asked, sitting down on a pool chair beside her friend.

Olivia shrugged. "Playing host, I guess," she said lightly.

Something in Olivia's expression made Elizabeth lean closer to her. "Is anything wrong?" she asked gently.

Olivia sighed and was silent for a long moment. "Oh, it's probably no big deal," she said finally. "I just feel like I made a fool out of myself, that's all."

"What do you mean?" Elizabeth asked.

Olivia shrugged again. Her voice was noncommittal, but her eyes looked full of hurt. "Well, to begin with, I showed up here about forty-five minutes early. Roger told me a few days ago that he wanted me to be early so he could show me around and introduce me to everyone before the rest of the guests came. And I guess I was a little nervous," she added. Elizabeth nodded understandingly.

"Well, I think Roger forgot all about asking me to come early. He was upstairs, getting dressed or something, when I showed up. Mrs. Patman answered the door, and—"

"What happened, Olivia?" Elizabeth prompted gently.

Olivia's face crumpled. "Oh, Liz, it was terrible," she whispered. "She just stared at me when she opened the door, and then she said something like 'And who might *this* be?' and she gave me a look like I was someone delivering packages or something."

"You can't let her get to you," Elizabeth said. "You're Roger's friend, and what she thinks doesn't matter. You'll see, Olivia."

"Oh, Liz," Olivia exclaimed. "I hope you're right!"

"Mrs. Patman, I'll get these for you," Jessica volunteered sweetly. Elizabeth had never seen her twin behave like this before. She had actually asked to be introduced to the other adults at the barbecue. Mr. Patman's client Mr. Ferguson and his wife were sitting under an umbrella in the shade, looking around them with

41

displeasure, and Jessica went so far as to sit down with them. Elizabeth walked past just as Mrs. Ferguson, pulling down her wide-brimmed hat, announced that teenagers today were the most inconsiderate creatures she had ever seen.

"I'm afraid I have to agree with you," Elizabeth had heard her twin say mournfully, clearly distinguishing herself from the inconsiderate teenagers milling all around them.

"You haven't said a single word to me all day," Neil Freemount complained, following Jessica as she moved from table to table, putting empty lemonade glasses onto a huge silver tray.

"Not now, Neil," Jessica hissed. "I want to give Mrs. Patman a hand with these dirty glasses," she said loudly, smiling past Neil at Mrs. Ferguson.

"Don't you think Jessica Wakefield is *so* lovely and poised?" Mrs. Patman wondered aloud. Roger, who was within earshot, didn't know whether or not he was supposed to answer her. "She's simply a pleasure to have around," Mrs. Patman added. "Roger, dear, tell me again the name of that little friend of yours who came here so early this morning."

"Olivia," Roger said, sighing. Talking to his aunt, he had decided, was not his favorite part of being a Patman.

"Olivia, dear? Do we know her family?"

"I don't think so, Aunt Marie," Roger mumbled.

"Mrs. Patman—excuse me—where can I put these?" Jessica interrupted, balancing the heavy tray of glasses awkwardly in her arms.

"Why, Jessica, how terribly *considerate* of you!" Mrs. Patman exclaimed. "Wasn't that considerate of her, Roger?" Mrs. Patman put a cool, perfectly manicured hand on Jessica's shoulder. "Why don't you just come with me, dear, and I'll show you where we're putting all the dishes. Will you excuse us, Roger?"

Jessica followed Mrs. Patman down the flagstone path to the side entrance of the kitchen. Her face felt stiff from smiling, and the tray was like a lead weight in her arms. *I sure hope Mrs. Patman appreciates this,* she thought, *or else I've wasted all this effort for nothing.*

"I can't *tell* you how helpful you've been, dear," Mrs. Patman said as Jessica set the tray down. "How would you like to have a glass of lemonade with me in the breakfast room, where it's cool, to refresh yourself?"

The last thing Jessica wanted was another glass of lemonade, but she hated to lose momentum now. "I'd love some," she said cheerfully.

Jessica followed Mrs. Patman into the enormous, oak-beamed room adjoining the kitchen. She took a seat across from Mrs. Patman at the large breakfast table.

"Here you are, dear," Mrs. Patman said, handing Jessica a tall glass of lemonade.

Jessica took a tiny sip and tried to look thrilled. "It's delicious," she managed.

Mrs. Patman leaned back in her chair and continued smiling at Jessica. In fact, she smiled so widely and for such a long time that Jessica began to wonder if something was wrong.

"It's so nice to get to meet all of Roger's friends before the party at the club," Mrs. Patman said at last, patting her hair with one hand. Jessica couldn't help noticing that the diamond ring on her left hand went all the way up to her knuckle. "Tell me," Mrs. Patman said suddenly, leaning forward across the table, "are you a very close friend of Roger's? We want so much, you see, to get to know his *real* friends."

"I wish we were closer." Jessica sighed and looked sweetly at Mrs. Patman. "Roger's so busy, you know. He studies so hard, and he's so serious about running."

"Yes, running," Mrs. Patman said, wrinkling her nose in distaste. "A dreadful habit, I think. We're hoping he'll take up something a little more social. Tennis would be nice, don't you think?" She sighed, patting her hair again. "Bruce is such a wonderful tennis player."

"Tennis is *my* favorite sport," Jessica said quickly.

Mrs. Patman's eyes narrowed. "Tell me, Jessica," she said, "who are Roger's really close friends, then? I want him to make sure he knows the right sort of people—now that he's part of the family."

44

"I'm not really sure," Jessica said evasively.

"Well, what about this Olivia, for instance?" Mrs. Patman asked. "Is she a friend of yours?"

"Uh—no, ma'am," Jessica said politely. "I've always thought Olivia is a little too shy," she added.

"I've thought so, too!" Mrs. Patman exclaimed, as if being shy were a criminal act. "Of course you're too sweet to say so, Jessica, but this Olivia is terribly awkward, isn't she? Not really the sort of girl who can help Roger very much, now that he has so much to learn—if you know what I mean," she added.

"I think I do," Jessica said, lowering her eyes.

Mrs. Patman smiled coolly at Jessica and set her glass down on the table. "We understand each other, don't we?" she asked sweetly. Before Jessica could answer, Mrs. Patman folded her hands together and continued. "I want so much for Roger to feel more at ease. It would be nice if he could find someone a little more suitable to spend his time with. Maybe you could help him, Jessica."

"That's very nice of you to say, Mrs. Patman," Jessica replied with mock innocence. "But I don't really see how—"

"For instance," Mrs. Patman interrupted, "I'd love to see you and Roger together two weeks from tonight at the party we're having at the club. I think you two would make such a lovely couple."

Jessica stood up, smiling. "I can't imagine anything I'd like more," she declared. Jessica was elated. Mrs. Patman wanted her to be Roger's date at the country club party! Jessica felt as if she'd won at least half the battle. *Now,* she told herself, *all I have to do is make Roger see how completely wrong Olivia is for him. And this afternoon,* Jessica thought to herself with a little smile, *looks like a good time to get to work.*

Five

Elizabeth was climbing out of the Patmans' pool, squeezing water from her blond ponytail, when she saw Lila Fowler and Caroline Pearce approach Regina across the patio. Regina had her back to the girls, and Lila tapped her on the shoulder to get her attention. *Time for some eavesdropping*, Elizabeth thought to herself, reaching for a towel. She dried herself off as slowly as possible, staying within earshot.

"Regina, I'm surprised you didn't bring that gorgeous man along with you today," Lila said coyly. "I was just telling Caroline how fabulous he is—that is, if you like older men," she added.

Regina flushed hotly. "I—I don't know what you mean," she stammered. "What man?"

Lila laughed, flicking her wavy, light brown hair off one shoulder. "Oh, come on, Regina," she said reprovingly. "Why would you want to keep it a secret? He looks just like Paul Newman," she told Caroline, who was listening avidly to every word.

Regina's eyes raced from Lila's lips to Caroline's as though she were afraid she might miss something. "Honestly, I don't know what you're talking about," she insisted.

Lila shook her head. "I think it's terribly unfair of you, Regina," she said coldly. "How can you hide him away from all of us? You're not ashamed of us, are you?" *Or of yourself*, Lila's expression said clearly.

Oh, dear, Elizabeth thought, hurrying over to rejoin Enid and Todd. *It looks like I was right about Lila. And now that Caroline Pearce is in on the story, Regina's secret will be all over Sweet Valley in a matter of days!*

"Hmm," Enid said after Elizabeth explained the situation to her. "So you two saw Regina downtown with some handsome older man, and you think Lila saw them at the same time you did?" Enid sat at the edge of the pool next to Elizabeth and Todd, and splashed water up onto her arms.

"I'm sure of it now," Elizabeth said sadly.

48

"What really worries me," she added, "is that Lila will tell more people than just Jessica and Caroline about it. It would be such a shame for Regina to be faced with a lot of stupid rumors. She's so new in Sweet Valley, and she's really a good person."

Enid looked puzzled. "You know I'm not exactly a Lila Fowler fan," she confessed, "but I'm not sure I understand why Lila would want to make trouble for Regina. What do you think she's up to, Liz?"

Elizabeth looked thoughtful as she whirled her long, tanned legs in the blue water. "I'm not exactly sure either, Enid," she admitted. "But to tell you the truth, I've gotten the impression that Lila hasn't exactly welcomed Regina with open arms. Maybe she feels a little threatened by her."

"Threatened by Regina?" Enid echoed.

"It makes sense," Todd declared. "Here Lila Fowler is, one of the richest girls in town, and pretty used to everyone knowing it. And then Regina moves in, and suddenly there's another rich girl in school."

"And a rich girl who also happens to be beautiful," Enid added.

"*And* nice," Elizabeth pointed out. "And also smart and charming."

"The plot thickens!" Enid exclaimed.

"I vote that we keep a close eye on the situation," Todd stated.

Elizabeth shook her head, her blond ponytail bouncing, "I don't think so, Todd," she told him. "I think we've gone far enough with our detective work. It isn't really any of our business, and we may actually make the whole situation worse if it looks like we're following her around. Lila probably guessed we were up to something already when she saw us downtown."

"Liz is right, Todd," Enid agreed.

Todd looked so disappointed that Elizabeth burst out laughing. "All right, Sherlock," she cried, splashing water at him. "We'll find another case to keep you happy!"

Todd laughed and leaned forward to rumple her hair.

"But in the meantime," Elizabeth said, growing serious again, "I think it's important that we show Regina we're on her side. If Lila Fowler really *is* trying to spread rumors about her, Regina's going to need all the friends she's got."

"Hey, aren't you three hungry?" George Warren, Enid's boyfriend, demanded. He had just come from the buffet table, and his paper plate was heaped with food.

"As a matter of fact, I'm starving," Todd announced, getting to his feet and reaching out to help Elizabeth up. "And if I know the Patmans, lunch will be fit for a king!"

Todd was right. The food arranged on the buffet table was an amazing sight—platters of hamburgers and hot dogs fresh from the barbecue grill, bowls of salad and coleslaw, every kind of fruit imaginable, from strawberries to melons to mangoes, and at the far end of the table, an array of mouth-watering desserts.

"I can't believe how good this looks!" Olivia exclaimed, standing behind Jessica in line.

"It does look pretty good," Jessica agreed, handing Olivia a paper plate and helping herself to a huge spoonful of salad.

Olivia took the spoon when she was done and wondered how much salad she should take. "You know, Jessica," she said, "I wish I could be more like you."

Jessica lifted a hamburger onto her plate with a fork and turned to stare at Olivia, who blushed under Jessica's penetrating blue-green gaze.

"You're so confident," Olivia explained. "I guess parties make me a little nervous."

Jessica realized she was still staring at Olivia, and with a start she turned back to the buffet table. After a moment's consideration, she chose a peach from the fruit basket, her mind racing. Jessica Wakefield had just had a flash of inspiration: Maybe the best way to get Olivia out of the picture would be to pretend to help Olivia stay *in* the picture. If Olivia really did admire her, it was up to Jessica to offer her advice. And, Jessica thought, a cunning little smile coming to her lips, it wouldn't really be *her* fault if the advice she offered Olivia didn't prove to be of much help at all.

"You should just relax," she told Olivia, taking a napkin and some plastic utensils from the end of the table. She flashed her most sincere smile, balancing her full plate easily in one hand.

"Do you think I should take dessert now?" Olivia asked, looking uncertainly at her plate.

Jessica thought for a minute. She hadn't seen anyone else take dessert yet. But Olivia *had* said she wanted to be more confident. "Of course," she said warmly. "Here, let me get you another plate."

"I don't know, Jessica," Olivia demurred. "Nobody else has two plates."

"Oh, come on, Olivia!" Jessica exclaimed impatiently. "This is a party. The only rule is that you be yourself and have a good time."

"Well, OK," Olivia said reluctantly, taking the second plate and filling it with fruit and chocolate brownies.

"Come on, let's go join the others," Jessica urged her, heading across the lawn to the tables under the brightly striped umbrellas. Olivia followed slowly behind her, carefully balancing her full plates of food.

"Jessica! Olivia! Over here," Neil Freemount called, jumping up from the table to pull out a chair for Jessica. Olivia followed her to the table, awkwardly maneuvering the two plates in her hands and looking helplessly at the one empty chair.

"Looks like you need help," Bruce said, apparently in no hurry to offer it. "Hey, look at that!" he exclaimed to the whole table, motioning at

Olivia's two plates. "Nothing like a girl with a good appetite."

"Let me help you, Olivia," Jessica said sweetly, bouncing out of her chair. Olivia turned bright red. Everyone was staring at her! Why couldn't she do anything right?

Jessica took both plates out of Olivia's hands and arranged them on the table. She made sure she took just long enough to make the moment especially awkward, and then she slipped back into her seat. *A friend in need is a friend indeed,* Jessica thought to herself, turning to Neil as if nothing had happened. But not before she had confirmed, out of the corner of her eye, that Roger looked as embarrassed as Olivia. Jessica smiled broadly at Neil as she reached for her hamburger. It looked as if her plan was off to a perfect start.

For the rest of the day, Jessica didn't let Olivia out of her sight. "Let's go swimming," she urged after everyone had waited the proper interval after lunch.

"I don't know," Olivia said uncertainly, looking back at Roger.

"Come on, Olivia," Jessica prompted under her breath. "Neil and Roger will follow us if we go get wet."

"OK," Olivia said, following Jessica to the pool. She stood at the edge of the pool shaking her head admiringly as she watched Jessica make a perfect dive from the diving board. Jessica looked so glamorous in her black one-piece! Suddenly Olivia wished she were wearing anything other than the old cotton bikini that Roger had seen a hundred times before.

Jessica surfaced, pushing her streaming blond hair out of her eyes. "Let's have a diving contest!" she called, treading water. Neil and Roger, just as she'd predicted, had followed the girls down to the pool.

"You're on!" Neil yelled, racing to the diving board.

Roger, standing beside Olivia, looked quizzically at her. "How's your diving?" he asked her.

Olivia swallowed. "I'm not sure I'd win any prizes," she admitted.

Roger smiled at her. "Come on," he said. "We don't want them to think we can't swim!"

Olivia didn't say anything. *Just be yourself*, Jessica had told her. But what if being herself wasn't good enough? she wondered. Roger dived neatly into the water, joining Jessica and Neil.

"Come on, Olivia!" Jessica yelled encouragingly, still treading water. Olivia looked down into the pool and sighed. *Oh, well, here goes nothing*, she thought, climbing up the diving board and walking slowly to the edge. She took a deep breath, stuck her arms out, and leaped. The next thing she knew she had hit the water full force with her belly. She had water in her mouth and her eyes, and she came to the surface sputtering and almost crying.

"Olivia, are you OK?" Jessica shouted,

swimming smoothly to her side. "Roger, she's hurt!" she yelled behind her.

Thanks to Jessica, several people around the pool jumped in to try and rescue Olivia.

"I'm OK," Olivia insisted as Roger and Neil helped her out of the pool.

"It's all my fault," Jessica said. "Olivia, I'm so sorry!"

"It's no one's fault, and I'm perfectly all right," Olivia said firmly. She smiled weakly at Roger. "I think I'm going to stick to sunbathing for the rest of the afternoon," she told him.

"I think that's a wonderful idea," Jessica agreed, squeezing the water out of her hair. "I'm going to go dry off," she announced, "if you're sure you're OK, Olivia."

"I'm fine," she insisted.

Jessica gave her one last parting smile and headed off across the lawn to the pool house. The afternoon was going even better than she'd hoped.

"Hey, Jess," Bruce Patman drawled, leaning against the pool house and looking approvingly at Jessica's figure in her sleek new suit. "If you're through with the aquatic act, how about a game of tennis?"

"No, thanks," Jessica said shortly. She had gotten Bruce out of her system ages ago, and the sight of him now made her face darken. "Don't the girls from college keep you busy enough these days?" she asked sarcastically.

"Come on, Jess," Bruce pleaded. "Let bygones be bygones, as they say. Just one quick game."

Jessica looked down at his racket, and a thought occurred to her. "Not now, Bruce," she told him, forcing herself to sound civil. "I'm really tired. Besides, it would be more fun to play doubles. Maybe another day."

"You're on!" Bruce cried. "Who do we play against?"

Jessica pretended to think it over. "What about your new cousin?" she asked innocently.

Now Bruce was the one to scowl.

"Come on, Bruce!" Jessica teased. "Are you afraid he'll show you up?"

"Are you kidding?" Bruce demanded, taking the bait.

As the captain of the tennis team, the last thing Bruce was worried about was losing to Roger at tennis. "Come to think of it," Bruce said, a smile playing about his lips, "maybe it wouldn't be so bad, playing with Roger."

"We'll need a fourth," Jessica reminded him. "Why don't we ask Olivia to play, too?"

Bruce looked at Jessica suspiciously. "I don't know what you're up to, Jess, but it sure sounds like you don't want much competition," he drawled.

Jessica grinned. "We'll go easy on them, won't we, Bruce?"

Bruce shook his head. "If you want to play with Roger and Olivia, we'll play with Roger and Olivia," he told her. "But I don't go easy on anyone."

Jessica shrugged. "Have it your way," she said lightly. "When shall we play?"

"Tuesday, after school," Bruce said. "You'd better give Olivia a few pointers before then," he added.

Oh, you can be sure of that, Jessica thought to herself with a little smile. "I'll leave it to you to set it up with Roger and Olivia," she told him, pushing past him into the pool house.

Jessica Wakefield, she told herself, catching a glimpse of her reflection in the full-length mirror inside, *you've got this one in the bag. Olivia isn't even going to know what hit her!*

Six

"Telephone, Jess!" Elizabeth announced, putting her hand over the receiver. "It's Olivia Davidson," she whispered, handing the receiver to her twin.

Jessica's face lit up. "Thanks, Liz," she said, grabbing the phone.

"Olivia!" she exclaimed, turning away from the puzzled expression on her sister's face. "How are you?"

The twins were downstairs in the Wakefields' comfortable family room, watching a movie on the brand-new videocassette recorder their father had installed the week before. Elizabeth turned the sound down on the set and plopped back down on the couch within earshot of her twin. Ordinarily Elizabeth was very respectful of her sister's privacy, but right now she had no intention of budging. *Something must be up*, she thought. Jessica and Olivia had spent most of the afternoon together the day before at the Patmans' barbecue, and Jessica had even seemed to go out of her way to look for Olivia. And much as Elizabeth loved her twin, she knew her too well to think Jessica would lavish so much attention on someone like Olivia unless she had an ulterior motive. *But what*, Elizabeth wondered, glancing uneasily at her twin, *could Jessica possibly want from Olivia Davidson?*

"Really? Tennis on Tuesday?" Jessica exclaimed, her face wrinkled up with theatrical surprise. "That sounds terrific, Olivia." She listened for a minute, then shook her blond head impatiently. "Don't give it a thought," she said emphatically. "I haven't played in ages myself. I'm sure I'll be rusty."

Elizabeth's ears pricked up. Jessica, rusty at tennis? Elizabeth was tempted to laugh, but her good sense warned her that this might not be a laughing matter. Jessica was a fabulous tennis player, and her unaccustomed modesty struck Elizabeth as distinctly strange.

"Oh, I don't know," Jessica was saying vaguely, twisting the telephone cord with one finger. "You don't really need to wear anything special. Hey, I know what!" she exclaimed, as if the thought had just come to her. "Let's go down to the mall tomorrow after school. I heard The Tennis Shop is having a sale."

Jessica listened for a minute longer, then smiled. "Terrific, Olivia," she said warmly. "I'll meet you there."

"What was that all about?" Elizabeth asked, punching the stop button on the remote control.

"Liz, what are you doing?" Jessica demanded, looking anguished. "We were just getting to the good part!"

"John Travolta can wait," Elizabeth said firmly. "I want to know why you've suddenly taken such an interest in Olivia Davidson."

Jessica shrugged. "Well, why shouldn't I?" she asked defensively. "You're not the only one who cares about other people, Elizabeth."

Elizabeth flushed hotly. She certainly didn't mean to make herself sound like the Good Samaritan. "OK, OK," she conceded. "But why does Olivia need your help all of a sudden?"

Jessica thought fast. "I think Lila Fowler is still after Roger," she said quickly. "And you know Lila—she's not exactly easy competition. So I just thought I'd give Olivia a few pointers. Lila doesn't deserve Roger, not after the way she treated him when she thought he was nothing but a janitor!"

"I agree with you there," Elizabeth admitted. "Still, I can't believe Lila is still interested in Roger, especially when it's so obvious how crazy Roger is about Olivia."

"You're absolutely right, Elizabeth," Jessica

agreed. "And all I'm trying to do is make sure Roger doesn't change his mind, now that he's a Patman."

"Well, that's awfully nice of you, Jess." Elizabeth shook her head, staring at her twin's innocent face. Maybe Jessica really was becoming more considerate of other people's feelings. All the same, Elizabeth couldn't suppress a twinge of uneasiness about her sister's new-found generosity. Was it possible Jessica had something else in mind other than good-natured friendship?

"*Now* can we watch the rest of the movie?" her twin demanded. Elizabeth sighed, pushing the play button and settling back on the couch. Apparently discussion was over.

Monday afternoon Elizabeth was lying back on the sprawling lawn in front of Sweet Valley High, enjoying the warmth of the sun. Enid and Todd were sitting close by. The last class of the day had just let out, and dozens of students were lounging on the grass, talking with their friends and taking a break before heading off for after-school activities.

Elizabeth sat up, shading her eyes with one hand. "Hey, Todd," she said, spotting a tall, handsome man in a gray business suit coming toward them, "isn't that the man we saw downtown with Regina?"

"It sure is," Todd confirmed.

The man had parked his car—a beautiful beige Ferrari—in the parking lot adjacent to the school before approaching the crowded lawn. He scanned the scene before him anxiously, as if he were looking for somebody.

"I wonder if he's trying to find Regina," Enid said.

"I don't see her anywhere," Todd said, glancing around the lawn.

"Uh-oh, we're not the only ones who've recognized him," Elizabeth said grimly.

Lila Fowler, who was on her way to the parking lot with Cara Walker, had turned around and was staring as the man walked up on the lawn. Then she went up to him and touched him on the arm.

"Can I help you find someone?" Elizabeth heard Lila ask sweetly.

"As a matter of fact, maybe you can," the man admitted. Closer up he was even handsomer than he had looked downtown the week before, Elizabeth thought. He had broad shoulders, a lean, athletic build, and dark, wavy hair just touched at the sideburns with silvery gray. And his eyes were a stunning shade of blue. "Do you know a girl named Regina Morrow?" the man asked Lila. "I was supposed to meet her here at three-thirty."

Just then Regina spotted him. "Hi, Lane!" she called, running up to him, her arms filled with books and her long hair flying.

The man smiled at Regina. "Let me take

those," he said protectively, reaching out for Regina's books. "Thanks for your help," he said to Lila. He and Regina walked across the lawn to the glinting beige Ferrari. Elizabeth and Todd exchanged looks of dismay as they watched him help Regina into the car. A minute later he had hopped in the driver's seat, and they were off.

"Wow," Todd said. "This must be Lila's lucky day."

Elizabeth shook her head ruefully. Sure enough, Lila was watching the departing car with a triumphant smirk on her pretty face.

"I wonder where those two are off to in such a hurry," Lila said pointedly, making sure her voice carried to the growing audience gathered on the lawn. Then she headed back to the parking lot, twirling her gold keychain in one hand. "Come on, Cara," she called haughtily.

"Was that *him*, Lila?" Caroline Pearce demanded, trying to catch up with the two girls.

Lila smiled imperiously at her. "It certainly was," she confirmed. As far as Lila was concerned, Regina Morrow had just done her own reputation enough damage to last a long time.

Olivia was waiting for Jessica outside The Tennis Shop at four o'clock sharp. "That's quite an interesting outfit you're wearing," Jessica told her, taking in every detail of Olivia's gauze wraparound skirt, Indian shirt, and leather sandals.

Olivia looked down at her clothes uneasily. A few weeks earlier she would have ignored any comment about the way she dressed, but these days she was increasingly touchy about her appearance. "Thanks," she said uncertainly. "I found this skirt at a thrift shop downtown."

"*Really*," Jessica remarked. "Well, let's see what kind of tennis clothes we can find in here."

Twenty minutes later Olivia came out of the dressing room, holding herself awkwardly in the starched white shorts and matching polo shirt Jessica had picked out for her to try on. "I don't know, Jessica," she said. "It just doesn't seem like *me*, somehow."

Jessica walked around Olivia and looked her up and down critically. "You may be right," she agreed. "I don't know, Olivia. Maybe you don't really need tennis clothes. They don't look quite right on you, do they?"

"I'm just going to wear my most comfortable pair of track shorts," Olivia declared.

"That's the spirit!" Jessica cried. "It doesn't matter *what* you wear as long as you feel good about it," she added.

Olivia shook her head at her reflection in the three-way mirror, her curly hair tumbling over her shoulders.

"Brooke Shields I'm not. That's for sure," she said, laughing. As she caught a glimpse of the price tag dangling from the shorts, she added to herself, *And I don't have her allowance, either.*

"Tomorrow will be fun no matter what,"

Jessica promised, following Olivia into the dressing room.

"I don't know, Jessica," Olivia said doubtfully, stepping carefully out of the shorts and clipping them back on the wire hanger. "I'm really not much of a tennis player. Are you *sure* you haven't played in ages?"

"Of course I'm sure," Jessica lied. "And I asked Bruce to go easy on all of us," she said, not mentioning Bruce's response to her request. "I told you, Olivia, all you have to do is relax and enjoy yourself." She took the polo shirt Olivia had removed and folded it neatly. "Besides," she added, her blue-green eyes sparkling conspiratorially, "you have to show the Patmans you can play on their terms." *And if you can't,* Jessica thought to herself, *isn't it better that Roger finds out now, so he can find someone who can? Someone,* she thought, catching a glimpse of herself in the dressing room mirror, *like me.*

"Let's stop in The Designer Shop for a minute," Jessica suggested as she and Olivia headed back out into the mall.

"Why?" Olivia asked her. "Isn't it a little expensive?"

"Oh, I don't know," Jessica said airily. "After all, you and Roger have a pretty special occasion coming up."

Olivia looked at her blankly. "You mean the party at the country club?"

"Of course!" Jessica burst out impatiently. "You know, Olivia, there'll be an awful lot of people there counting on you and Roger to make just the right impression."

"I guess so," Olivia muttered. She hadn't really thought of it that way before. As a matter of fact, Olivia had been saving money from baby-sitting, and just the week before, she had bought some beautiful fabric from a sewing shop downtown. She'd planned to design and sew a dress herself. The one thing she had hoped was that her dress would be entirely original. She hadn't really thought what kind of impression it would make.

"Now, this would look beautiful on you!" Jessica cried, fingering a filmy strapless gown on display inside The Designer Shop. Olivia looked around her nervously. Stores like this made her distinctly uncomfortable. A lot of times you couldn't tell which was a salesgirl and which a mannequin! Olivia touched the dress Jessica had pointed out, trying to look enthusiastic. As she fingered the soft material, her eyes fell on the price tag dangling from the bodice of the dress. Olivia caught her breath in amazement. *Two hundred and ninety dollars!* Who in the world could afford to spend that kind of money on a dress that could be worn only once or twice? "I don't think so, Jessica," she said firmly.

Jessica didn't answer. She followed Olivia out of the store and waited until they had walked a bit to make her next move. "You know, Olivia," she said, "maybe I shouldn't tell you this, but I overheard Roger saying something to Todd the other day—"

"What was it?" Olivia asked quickly.

Jessica shrugged. "Oh, it probably didn't mean a thing," she said lightly. "I'm sure it was just one of those things that came into his head and then he forgot all about."

"Jessica, *tell* me," Olivia demanded, looking anguished.

Jessica sighed. "All right, Liv, if you really want me to," she said reluctantly. "Roger told Todd that he was having a really hard time lately with his aunt. He said things would be much easier if you—well, *you* know, Olivia—if you cared about the sort of things most people do. Like clothes, for instance."

Olivia stared at Jessica, her face going very pale. "Did he say anything else?" she demanded.

Jessica shook her head. "But you know, Liv," she said gently, "maybe you should think more about Roger's feelings. It might make things a lot easier for him if you thought about what kind of dress he'd like you to buy."

Jessica has a point, Olivia thought. *Maybe Roger needs me to be different now that he's a Patman. Maybe he needs me to look different and act different.*

Or maybe, she thought, feeling a flash of embarrassment, *he needs someone he doesn't have to feel ashamed of in front of his new family. Maybe I'm not right for Roger Patman after all.*

67

Seven

"One good thing about the lunches they serve around here," Lila Fowler said grumpily, pushing her Hungarian goulash around with her fork, "is that they make dieting a little easier. I don't know how you can eat like that, Jessica, and still stay so slim!"

Jessica popped one last french fry in her mouth and reached for her carton of chocolate milk. "I need energy, Lila, dear," she reminded her friend. "I'm facing fierce competition on the Patman courts this afternoon!"

Lila giggled. "You're too much." Lowering her voice a little, she said, "Frankly, I hope your little scheme works. It makes me sick watching

Roger and Olivia together. I can't imagine what he sees in her."

"I have a feeling he won't be seeing her at all much longer," Jessica said and laughed. She finished her last gulp of milk and leaned her head closer to Lila's. "Don't say a word to anyone, but I'll bet that Roger suddenly experiences a change of heart and decides to ask someone else to the dance at the country club."

"And I wonder who that might be?" Lila said slyly. "Speaking of dates for the dance," she added, "I wonder if Regina Morrow plans to show up with her middle-aged Mystery Man."

"Tell me what happened yesterday," Jessica demanded. "I can't believe I missed the whole thing."

Lila shook her head reprovingly. "It was just amazing, Jess," she confided. "They were all *over* each other! Frankly, I'm a little surprised at Regina," she added. "Everyone knows what older men are like. I'm sure they didn't go off to do her homework!" She giggled.

"Lila, you don't really think she's—"

"Well, what else could it be?" Lila interrupted airily. "If you'd seen them, Jess, you'd be as sure as I am."

"Seen who?" Caroline Pearce demanded, bringing her tray over and sliding into the seat next to Lila.

"No one," Jessica said firmly. Letting Caroline in on a secret was about as safe as printing it on a billboard.

69

"Actually," Lila declared, spreading her hands out and admiring her perfectly manicured nails, "we were talking about Regina and her new man."

"Really?" Caroline asked eagerly. "What about him?"

Jessica looked at Lila with some surprise. *She must really want the word to get out,* Jessica thought, *if she's telling Caroline about it.*

Lila shrugged. "You know older men," she said mysteriously. "I'm just surprised Regina's got such a wild streak in her. They probably won't go to the Patmans' party after all," she continued, running her fingers through her hair. "They probably have other things to do."

Caroline gasped. "I can't believe it." She looked from Jessica to Lila and shook her head.

Nothing like a little negative publicity, Lila thought happily. She was sure that by the end of the day Caroline would have told everyone in Sweet Valley High that Regina Morrow was in terrible trouble.

"Speaking of the Patmans' party, who are you two going with?" Caroline inquired.

"Who knows," Lila said, looking as if she couldn't imagine a more boring question.

"We're going to keep them all guessing," Jessica added, giggling.

Caroline looked from one to the other, then sighed deeply. "Too bad Adam can't make it," she said mournfully.

"Who's Adam?" Lila asked. As far as she knew, Caroline had never had a date in her life.

"Oh, Lila, he's wonderful," Caroline gushed, pushing her red hair back with one hand. Her green eyes sparkled with excitement. "He lives about two hours from here in Cold Springs. That's why he can't make it to the party at the country club," she explained. "He can't arrange to be away that weekend."

"How'd you meet him if he lives so far away?" Jessica asked.

"Oh, we met at a party my parents gave. His father used to work with my father, but we never met until about a month ago. Jessica, he's so handsome! He's really tall, and he's got an incredible build—"

"It must be hard to get to know him if he lives so far away," Lila commented.

"Oh, it is. It's torture," Caroline agreed. "But Adam writes amazing letters. In fact, he's been writing me almost every day. He calls a lot, too," she added, "but his letters are the best. They're *so* romantic. Adam's just fantastic."

"Well, when do we get to meet this dream man?" Lila demanded.

"Soon," Caroline said, smiling serenely. "He says he can't bear to be away from me much longer."

"Who ever would have believed that Caroline Pearce could get a boyfriend?" Lila demanded as she and Jessica walked up to the counter to put their trays away.

71

"Things sure are getting stranger by the minute around here," Jessica agreed.

"Let's go sit with Regina," Elizabeth suggested to Todd, spotting the girl sitting by herself across the cafeteria.

"OK," Todd said, grinning. The two made their way over to Regina, but before they could put their trays down, Caroline Pearce had approached her from the other side. "It's not true, is it, Regina?" Elizabeth heard her ask. "Why in the world would you want to get so involved with someone old enough to be your father?"

Regina got to her feet, her face flaming to the roots of her hair.

"Regina, please stay," Elizabeth begged, speaking directly to the deaf girl so Regina could read her lips. "Todd and I were going to join you."

"Sorry, I've got to run," Regina mumbled, knocking her chair over in her haste to get past them.

"Boy, she's really on edge," Todd commented, watching Regina hurry out of the lunchroom, her eyes to the ground.

Elizabeth shook her head. "I'm afraid all this nonsense is really getting to her, Todd. I just wish there was something we could do to help." She looked down at her tray and shook her head. "I don't feel very hungry anymore," she admitted. Todd reached across the table and squeezed her hand.

"We'll think of something," he promised.

Elizabeth picked up her fork and poked listlessly at her food. What in the world could they do?

Just on time, Jessica said to herself, checking her reflection in the rearview mirror of the red Fiat. She had parked the car in the side drive near the Patmans' garage, and as she looked up, she saw Roger and Olivia walking toward her across the front lawn. Olivia, Jessica noticed with satisfaction, was wearing a pair of faded navy-blue track shorts and a baggy T-shirt. *Thank heavens Lila let me borrow this*, Jessica thought, smoothing the front of her tennis dress and admiring her long, tanned legs.

"Hi, Roger!" Jessica said happily, leaping out of the car. "Hi, Olivia," she added. "Where's Bruce?"

"He's down at the courts already, hitting a few balls," Roger explained.

"Roger's been giving me a tour," Olivia said dryly.

Jessica looked at Olivia more closely. Was it her imagination, or did she detect a sour note in the girl's voice?

"This estate is just so beautiful," Roger said enthusiastically. "Every time I think I've gotten used to it I find something I hadn't noticed before."

"I've always loved this place," Jessica said, looking around at the gently rolling lawns, the huge shade trees, and the spectacular facade of the Patman mansion.

"Let's go down and meet Bruce," Olivia said. Jessica thought by now that she sounded distinctly cross.

Bruce was down the hill on the red clay courts, practicing his serve. Like Jessica and Roger, he was dressed all in white.

"Maybe I should have bought that tennis outfit," Olivia whispered to Jessica.

"Don't be silly," Jessica told her. "You look fine."

"Ready for some stiff competition, Rog?" Bruce said, throwing his racket up in the air and catching it neatly in the same hand.

"Let's play men against women first," Jessica said quickly. "Come on, Olivia."

"I guess that means old Rog is my partner," Bruce said with a grimace.

"Come on, Olivia," Jessica called, running across the beautiful clay courts. "We'll show them a thing or two."

"Just try not to make a complete fool of yourself," Bruce advised Roger cheerfully, picking his racket up and facing the net.

"Jessica," Olivia said anxiously, "I'm not sure I'm ready for a game yet. Shouldn't we warm up first?"

"We're only playing for fun," Jessica reminded her. "Don't worry," she added. "If the shots are hard, I'll get them for you."

Olivia picked up her racket uneasily. *Oh, dear,* Jessica thought to herself; *she really is a beginner. She looks as if she's holding a baseball bat.*

Bruce served first, smashing the ball with all his strength over the net. Olivia swatted her racket valiantly but missed the ball by about a mile. Face flaming, she chased after it.

"Good try," Jessica said kindly.

"Liv, try to stand this way," Roger called, bending his knees in an exaggerated stance.

"She's doing just fine," Jessica defended.

The first game, Jessica thought, was a complete success. Olivia missed every shot over the net. Her face went all red and sweaty, and it looked as though a big blister was forming on her right hand. Every time Olivia missed, Roger yelled something instructive at her, and Jessica could sense Olivia's growing frustration. "Just ignore him," Jessica told her as they got ready for the second game.

"You didn't tell me you were so good," Olivia said, wiping her brow.

"Oh," Jessica said, looking genuinely embarrassed. "I guess I'm not as rusty as I thought I'd be. It's funny how it sticks with you," she added.

"I don't think it'll ever stick with me," Olivia muttered.

"I'll tell you what," Jessica suggested. "I'll

75

take all the hard shots. Just step out of the way a little if a hard one comes."

"Sure thing," Olivia said, wiping her hand on her shorts.

During the second game Jessica rushed for every shot, delivering them with perfect speed and accuracy over the net. "Not bad, Jess," Bruce called admiringly. "Why can't *you* do that?" he muttered to Roger.

"I'm doing what I can, cousin," Roger said cheerfully.

"We'll show them in the next game," Jessica said triumphantly. Olivia, she thought, looked exhausted. Her hair was hanging in little strings from the heat, and her face was bright red from exertion. "How many games do we play?" Olivia gasped.

"Just six," Jessica told her.

"Maybe we should switch teams," Roger suggested. "I can give you some tips, Liv."

Olivia looked furious. "Let's just stay as we are," she said woodenly.

"I can see now why Aunt Marie is so crazy about tennis," Roger said happily. "This is a lot of fun."

"Fun for you, maybe," Bruce muttered, "but I'm the one who's doing all the work."

"Don't worry," Jessica told Olivia. "Let's keep going the way we did last game. I'll take the hard ones."

Olivia sighed and picked up her racket again. *Now*, Jessica thought, *the time has come to change strategy*. Instead of taking every shot, as she had in the last game, Jessica rushed for most of them. But just when Olivia began to rely on her to cover the ball, Jessica fell back, crying, "It's yours, Olivia!" By this point Olivia was so confused she had no idea what to do. Bruce's final serve of the game was so devastating that Olivia tripped trying to get it, falling forward on the hard clay.

"Liv!" Jessica shrieked, suddenly all worry and compassion. "Are you all right?"

Olivia got to her feet slowly, her face wet with perspiration and tears. "I'm all right," she said quietly. "I think I just skinned my hands a little."

"Maybe we should take a break," Jessica suggested.

Roger's face fell. "You don't want to stop, do you, Liv?" he asked.

Olivia shrugged. "I don't care," she said, her lower lip trembling.

"I think we should stop," Jessica insisted. "You were terrific," she told Olivia. "Wasn't she terrific? I don't know if I could have played that well when I first started."

"Thanks for being so patient," Olivia told them all. "I think it's time for me to go home and recover."

Roger looked crushed. "You really want to stop, Liv? I thought you were doing so much better than last game."

"Yes, Roger," Olivia said firmly. "I think I *do* want to stop."

"I'll drive you home, Liv," Jessica offered quickly. *There's no point letting the two of them have a minute alone together*, she thought to herself, *not when I've worked so hard to make sure everything turned out so dismally.*

"Thanks, Jess," Olivia said. "Well, thanks for the game," she said to Roger. She didn't smile when she said it, and Roger didn't smile back.

"I don't know what it is about boys and sports," Jessica said, dropping Olivia off in front of her house. "They get so ridiculously *serious* about the whole thing."

"Thanks, Jess," Olivia repeated, getting out of the car. She shook her head then, smiling. "It wasn't your fault I was such a disaster," she added.

Jessica smiled to herself as she drove away. *"Fault" isn't the word I'd choose*, she thought. *"Credit" is more like it, and the credit is all mine.*

Eight

"Liz, can I ask you for a favor?" Regina Morrow said quietly, slipping up to Elizabeth, who had stopped at her locker between classes. Elizabeth pulled out her French book, then turned to face the other girl.

"Sure, Regina," she answered. "What is it?"

Regina glanced around uncomfortably. "Have you heard some of the things people are saying about me?" she asked. Her beautiful face looked unhappy and perplexed.

"As a matter of fact, I have," Elizabeth said truthfully. "But I know it's all complete nonsense."

79

Regina shook her head sadly. "Elizabeth, I have to talk to you," she said urgently. "What are you doing after school today?"

"Well—" Elizabeth took one look at the unhappy girl and decided that her "Eyes and Ears" column would have to be put off again. "Nothing," she said cheerfully. "What do you have in mind?"

"Would you come home with me after school?" Regina begged her. "Just for an hour or two. Oh, Liz, I need to talk to someone so badly!"

"Of course I'll come," Elizabeth assured her. "Why don't I meet you on the lawn after our last class gets out?"

"Liz, thank you so much," Regina said gratefully. She shook her head, and her long, dark hair moved gently from side to side. "Boy, you can sure tell who your real friends are at a time like this!" she exclaimed, smiling wryly past Elizabeth as Lila Fowler hurried by with her nose in the air.

"What was that all about?" Todd demanded, catching up to Elizabeth in the hall and slipping his arm around her waist. "I just saw Regina leaving your locker."

"Oh, Todd," Elizabeth said, "I'm so worried about her. I think the rumors people are spreading are really starting to get her down."

80

Todd shook his head sympathetically. "Anything we can do to help her out?" he asked her.

Elizabeth smiled up at him gratefully. "Did I ever tell you that you happen to be a pretty sensitive guy—in addition to all your other good qualities?"

"That's me," Todd said, laughing and giving Elizabeth a quick hug. "Just call me Boy Wonder!"

"I'm not really sure *what* we can do," Elizabeth said thoughtfully. "Regina just invited me to go over to her house after school. She says she wants to talk."

"Well, I can't think of a better shoulder to cry on," Todd said fondly. The first bell rang, and Todd jumped. "I better run," he said. "I've got a math quiz this period. Give me a call tonight and let me know what happened," he urged, giving her hand a quick squeeze. Elizabeth smiled as she watched him bounding down the hall. He was so handsome, she thought. Then she turned and went to her French class. She slid into her seat a minute before the last bell rang, took her notes out, and tried to focus on them. What in the world did Regina have to tell her? Would she explain what had been going on with the handsome older man? Elizabeth shook her head, looking back down at her notes. It sure was going to be hard to concentrate the rest of the day.

"Let's go up to my room," Regina suggested,

leading Elizabeth through the cool, high-ceilinged foyer.

Elizabeth looked around her admiringly. The Morrows had moved to Sweet Valley recently, buying one of the great mansions on the hill near the Patmans' estate. It was funny, Elizabeth thought, following Regina up the graceful grand staircase leading to the second floor, how much more like a home the Morrow estate felt than the Patmans'. It was certainly as big, but the sunshine spilling through the windows, the numerous plants, and the warm colors of curtains and carpeting all helped to make the great rooms seem less imposing, even cozy.

At the top of the stairs a door opened, and Nicholas Morrow, Regina's eighteen-year-old brother, stepped out into the hall. "Oh, hello, Elizabeth," he said, his face lighting up when he saw the Wakefield twin beside his sister. "I thought I heard someone come in."

Elizabeth smiled back. "Hi, Nicholas," she said warmly. It was hard not to like Nicholas Morrow. His emerald-green eyes flashed with good humor, and his jet black hair, bright smile, and broad physique had already won him quite a few admirers in Sweet Valley. When the Morrows had first moved in, Jessica Wakefield had made a big play for Nicholas. Much to her chagrin, it turned out that Nicholas had preferred Elizabeth. Elizabeth had not been immune to Nicholas Morrow's good looks and ready charm; and she had gone out on a date with him.

When Todd had found out about Elizabeth and Nicholas, he'd almost broken up with her. But all that was behind them now, and the two had remained friends even after Nicholas realized that Elizabeth's affection and loyalty remained with Todd.

"What are you two doing inside on such a gorgeous day?" Nicholas asked curiously.

"We might ask you the same thing, Nicholas," Regina teased. No one was a greater fan of Nicholas Morrow's than his younger sister, whose face had brightened the minute he opened his door. "Elizabeth's offered to help me with my chemistry," she added.

"Ah, now there's a good cause." Nicholas grinned. "I'm doing some work in here myself," he added, "but let me know if I can dazzle either one of you with my science skills."

Regina and Elizabeth laughed and continued down the hall to Regina's room. "I didn't want to trouble Nicholas with any of the stuff that's been going on at school," Regina explained, hanging her jacket up and plopping down on a huge, comfortable chair covered with pastel-flowered material.

Elizabeth settled down on the cream-colored couch across from her. "What a beautiful room, Regina!" she exclaimed. A tall canopy bed stood in the center of the room, which had been decorated in pastels. Gauzy curtains were moving in the breeze at the two enormous windows, and the whole room looked as soft and delicate as the inside of a flower.

"I did most of the decorating myself," Regina admitted shyly. "I guess I've always been interested in color and design." She shook her head. "In a way, that's how this whole mess with Lane Townsend got started!"

Townsend? Elizabeth thought. The name sounded familiar, but she wasn't sure why. "What do you mean?" she prompted.

Regina tucked her legs under her and took a deep breath, smoothing her cotton skirt with both hands. "Well, one day, soon after we'd moved in, I was downtown with my mother, looking for fabric to cover the couch you're sitting on. My mother had a few errands to run, and I was waiting for her outside. Elizabeth, the strangest thing happened!" Regina's face turned a little pink as she remembered.

Elizabeth leaned forward, her eyes riveted on Regina's.

"This man came up to me and introduced himself," Regina went on. "He gave me a business card and said his name was Lane Townsend and he ran a modeling agency."

"*That's* why the name sounded familiar!" Elizabeth exclaimed. "The Lane Townsend Agency is one of the best modeling agencies on the West Coast!"

"I know," Regina said. "That's why this whole thing seemed so strange to me. This is so embarrassing, Liz," she added. "I feel silly telling you this story, but I care so much about what you think, and I just couldn't stand the thought that *you* might believe any of those ridiculous rumors."

"Oh, Regina, I didn't believe them for a second," Elizabeth assured her.

"Well, anyway," Regina said, getting back to her story, "Lane gave me his card and told me he'd been running a contest for the last few months at his agency. He'd been trying to find a girl to model for a special story in *Ingenue* magazine. And—if you can believe it—he thought I was perfect for the job!"

"How wonderful!" Elizabeth exclaimed, looking at Regina with delight.

"So that's what happened," Regina concluded. "I had to get special permission to leave school early a few times for the shooting sessions. It's a good thing they're all over now," she admitted. "I was beginning to get behind in English."

"I'm sure Todd can lend you his notes," Elizabeth assured her. "And you're really going to be in *Ingenue?*"

Regina blushed again. "Believe it or not, Liz," she said, "I'm going to be on the cover of next month's issue!"

Elizabeth laughed with disbelief. "Why haven't you told anyone?" she demanded.

"I don't know." Regina sighed. "I feel a little funny about the whole thing. I guess I thought it would be better to let everyone find out when the magazine comes out. And of course, I had no idea people would make such a fuss about Lane. Not that he isn't gorgeous," she admitted, laughing. "But, Liz, he's happily married! The only time I saw him outside the agency was one afternoon last week when I agreed to baby-sit for Simone, his little daughter. Lane and his wife had to go to a big dinner out of town, and their regular sitter canceled at the last minute." She shook her head, still smiling. "Not a very romantic date," she said wryly.

"Regina, I'm so excited for you," Elizabeth told her proudly. "When does the magazine come out?"

"In the next week or two, I think," Regina said. Her face turned serious again, and she leaned forward in the chair. "Liz, please don't say anything until it does. I know it seems silly, but all my life I've tried to show people that I can fight my own fights if I have to. If anyone wants to believe those stupid rumors, let them. They'll find out the truth soon enough."

Elizabeth swallowed. It was going to be pretty hard to keep this secret from Todd, and the thought of lying to him made her uneasy. But she saw how important it was to Regina not to tell anyone. "I promise," she said. "My lips are sealed!"

"How'd the chemistry go?" Nicholas demanded, sticking his head out the door as Elizabeth and Regina were about to head downstairs.

"Not bad," Regina told him, smiling at Elizabeth. "Liz is a terrific tutor. But if you're still interested," she added, "there's one or two weak points I saved for you."

"My periodic chart awaits you!" Nicholas said grandly.

"I can't wait to see that magazine," Elizabeth told Regina as they said goodbye at the front door. "Does your family know?"

Regina stopped short. "Actually, they do," she told Elizabeth. "It's kind of a long story. I didn't tell my mother about it until I knew for sure that *Ingenue* would run the cover."

"Why not?" Elizabeth asked her.

"Well, my mother used to be a model herself," Regina said slowly. "In fact, she was a very well-known cover girl in New York when she met my father. She kept on with it for a while, but before I was born, she decided to give it up completely. She never told me this, but it turns out that ever since I was born, she hoped I'd model one day."

"What did she say when she found out?" Elizabeth asked.

Regina looked down at the ground, her face flushing. "She was very happy," she said softly. "I think it made a lot of things easier for her. You see, she was taking medication before I was born, and the doctors think that may have caused my deafness."

"Oh, no," Elizabeth said softly.

Regina smiled, her face clearing. "Anyway, I think the modeling became a kind of symbol for her of something she'd done that I could never do. I don't think I've ever seen her as happy as the day I told her about the magazine cover."

"Oh, Regina, I'm so happy for you," Elizabeth said, hugging her impulsively.

"But my mother's been sworn to secrecy!" Regina laughed. "She hasn't been able to tell a single one of her friends, and I think she's about to die. I think everyone will feel a lot better once this is finally out in the open."

You're not kidding, Elizabeth thought to herself, stepping outside into the brilliant afternoon sunshine. She could think of at least one person who was going to have a lot of questions in the meantime.

"What do you mean, you can't tell me what she said?" Todd demanded into the phone.

Elizabeth was in her bedroom with the door shut, lounging on her bed with the receiver cupped to her ear. Jessica was downstairs baking chocolate cookies, her latest brainstorm for the cheerleaders' crusade to earn money.

"I told you, Todd," Elizabeth repeated guiltily, "Regina made me swear not to tell a soul. She said she's not involved with that man, but I can't tell you what's going on yet. But Todd, it's so wonderful!"

"You're sure you can't tell me?" Todd asked. "It doesn't seem fair, really."

"I promise, Todd, you'll be so happy when

you find out what it is," Elizabeth said gently. "And I can't really go back on my word to Regina, can I?"

"I guess not," Todd said.

"The main thing," Elizabeth added, "is that she knows we're both on her side."

"Mmm," Todd said noncommittally.

After she hung up the phone, Elizabeth lay on her bed for a minute, her mind whirling with the story Regina had told her. She was glad Regina felt that she could trust her, but at the same time Elizabeth hated holding out on Todd. *I just hope I did the right thing*, she thought to herself, pulling herself up and jumping off the bed. One thing was certain, she thought. When *Ingenue* magazine came out with Regina's picture on the cover, her undercover partner was in for a big surprise.

Nine

"Is anything wrong, Olivia?" Elizabeth asked, leaning back in her chair and resting her hands on the typewriter. She and Olivia were the only ones working after school that afternoon in the *Oracle* office.

"I'm just having a hard time concentrating these days," Olivia admitted, shaking her head over the sheaf of papers in her hand.

Elizabeth swiveled in her chair to face Olivia. Come to think of it, Olivia *did* look tired. She was a little paler than usual, and there were faint circles under her eyes.

"Liz, can I ask you something?" Olivia said suddenly.

"Sure," Elizabeth told her. "I'm afraid I'm not getting much done today, either." *That's because all I can think of for the "Eyes and Ears" column is that a certain girl suspected of having an illicit affair is about to become a cover girl,* she thought to herself.

"Tell me the truth, Liz," Olivia went on, getting out of her chair and coming over to the window. "Do you think I dress strangely?"

Elizabeth stared at her, her brow wrinkling in surprise. "What are you talking about?" she demanded.

"No, I mean it, Liz," Olivia insisted. "Look at me. Do I dress like a freak?"

Elizabeth took a good look at Olivia, who was wearing oversized army pants, sandals, and a bright-yellow T-shirt with the sleeves rolled up. Her usual bandana was twisted into a thin band around her forehead, holding her froth of brown curls out of her eyes. "No, you don't, Olivia," Elizabeth said firmly. "You dress like yourself, and I think you look fabulous."

Olivia sighed. "Thanks, Liz," she said, turning around and going back to her chair.

"Why did you ask?" Elizabeth inquired. "It's funny, Olivia, but you never struck me as being worried about what other people think about the way you dress."

"Oh, I don't know," Olivia said. "I was just curious." Something in her voice made Elizabeth think the discussion was over.

"Hey, this is something you might be interested in, Liz," Olivia said, handing Elizabeth a typewritten sheet of paper.

"Junior playwriting competition," Elizabeth read aloud. "Mr. Jaworski, Sweet Valley High's drama coach, is pleased to announce Sweet Valley's annual junior playwriting competition. This year's theme is famous literary figures. Interested students should submit an original one-act play to Mr. Jaworski no later than . . ." Elizabeth stared at the date and realized with a start that it was only one month away.

"You're right, Olivia. I am interested. Thanks," Elizabeth said, handing her friend the paper. "But if I'm going to enter this contest, I'd better start working right away."

Just then the door to the *Oracle* office opened, and Jessica burst in. "Fifty-five dollars exactly!" she announced triumphantly. "And you said no one would buy those cookies because they looked so weird. Just shows how much *you* know about business, Liz."

"Jessica!" Elizabeth exclaimed. "What a surprise. What brings you to the world of journalism? Do you have any great gossip for my column?" she asked hopefully.

"Not a word," Jessica said cheerfully. She looked around the crowded office and wrinkled her nose distastefully. "Ugh," she complained. "This place is a mess. What's all that paper?"

Elizabeth laughed. "That *paper*," she pointed out, "is the layout for the *Oracle*, Jess." Elizabeth turned to Olivia, who was gathering her books and papers together and stuffing them into her backpack. "Jessica doesn't seem to think we're tidy in here." She giggled, thinking about the usual state of her sister's bedroom.

Olivia looked around the office and sighed. "Well, it *is* kind of a mess, Liz," she admitted. Elizabeth thought her voice sounded a bit strained. It was hard to tell whether Olivia was glad to see Jessica or not.

"Ready, Liv?" Jessica asked.

Olivia nodded. "Jessica's offered to help me hem the dress I'm making for the Patmans' party," she told Elizabeth.

Elizabeth's eyes widened. "Jessica? But—"

"Yes, Liz," Jessica said quickly. "Tell Mom I'll be home in time for dinner."

Elizabeth couldn't believe her ears. The last time she'd seen her sister with a needle and thread was when she'd been forced to help string popcorn one year at Christmas.

"See you tomorrow, Liz," Olivia said, following Jessica out the door.

"Sure, Liv," Elizabeth answered, staring at her sister's retreating back. Since when, Elizabeth wondered, had Jessica turned into Betsy Ross? She didn't know a thing about sewing!

In fact, Elizabeth thought, *Jessica seems to be awfully eager to help Olivia with just about everything these days.* She turned back to her typewriter. *Oh, well*, Elizabeth thought philosophically, *I've poked my nose in other people's business enough as it is. Whatever Jessica is up to this time, I'm going to stay far away.*

"Here it is," Olivia said uncertainly, spreading the dress out on her bed and stepping back from it. "What do you think?"

"Hmm," Jessica said thoughtfully, touching the material with a practiced hand. "Is it"—she thought for a minute—"cotton?"

Olivia nodded unhappily. The fabric that had struck her as so beautiful when she'd chosen it now looked perfectly ordinary. It was pale lilac, a color Olivia had always loved, with tiny white flowers embossed on it. "It comes from Greece," she told Jessica, waiting anxiously for her reaction.

Only Olivia Davidson would dream of wearing a dress like this to the country club, Jessica thought. The dress didn't seem to have much shape to it, though it was certainly long enough. Olivia had designed a deep neckline that plunged in a vee, and had made a soft, gathered sash in the same material to cover the waistline. The dress was sleeveless, and actually, Jessica thought, walking around the bed to get a good look at it, it wouldn't look half bad as a bathing suit cover-up. But to wear to the biggest party of the season? She shuddered at the thought.

"What do you think?" Olivia repeated, her throat dry.

"Well . . . I think it's incredibly original,

94

Olivia," Jessica said carefully. "It's very simple, isn't it?" she asked.

"Yes, I was hoping it would be," Olivia said. "I've always hated those really fussy dresses they sell in stores."

"Hmm," Jessica said. "Why don't you put it on, Liv, and I'll help you with the hem? I'm sure it looks totally different when it's on you," she added.

Olivia went into the small bathroom next to her room and emerged a minute later, wearing the dress.

"So what do you think?" she asked softly. "Tell me the truth."

Jessica sighed. "I don't know, Olivia," she said thoughtfully, pretending to scrutinize the dress from all angles. "It's a beautiful dress," she added quickly, "but it just seems a little informal to me, don't you think?"

Olivia's face fell. "What do you mean?"

Jessica got up and walked around her, shaking her head. "Olivia," she said at last, "you have to remember how important this party is for Roger. After all, it's his first big event as a Patman. Everyone will be looking at him, and that means everyone will be looking at you, too."

"I know," Olivia said miserably. "I'm beginning to get that impression."

"And what that means," Jessica said firmly, "is that you have to think about Roger's feelings. You know how Mrs. Patman is," she pointed out. "She always makes such a big fuss about the stupidest things. In fact," Jessica added, dropping her voice confidentially, "Bruce told me once that she made one of his dates cry because the poor girl didn't know how to eat lobster. She absolutely traumatized her right in the middle of the Palomar House!"

"So what am I supposed to do?" Olivia demanded.

Jessica pretended to think it over. "Liv, I think it's wonderful that you tried to make this dress all by yourself," she told her. "But maybe the Patmans' party isn't the best place for it. After all," she added, "Roger isn't the only one people will be looking at. It'll be *your* first big event as Roger Patman's girlfriend, and you don't want people to think that you just threw on any old thing in your closet."

Olivia went very pale. "Thanks, Jessica," she said, going back into the bathroom to take the dress off. "You've been a big help."

"I've got a great idea," Jessica said when Olivia returned. "Why don't we go over to the mall and try to find something a little dressier? As a matter of fact, I have to look for something to wear myself," she added.

"Maybe later, Jess," Olivia said wearily. "I've got tons of homework to do tonight."

Jessica was quiet for a minute. "All right, Liv," she said, getting up and going to the bedroom door. She paused, trying to think of the best thing to say in parting. "It's up to you," she told

Olivia. "But don't you think this is a little more important than homework?"

Olivia stared at her. "What are you talking about?" she demanded.

Jessica shook her head. "This is probably going to be one of the biggest nights of Roger's life!" she exclaimed. "Don't you see, Liv—everything depends on you. The Patmans are all Roger has anymore. They're his family. All I'm saying," Jessica concluded, "is that Roger's depending on you to help him make the right sort of impression. And if you let him down . . ." She let her voice trail off, her expression filled with horror at the imagined consequence.

"Thanks for coming over, Jessica," Olivia said firmly, walking down the hallway, clearly hinting that she wanted Jessica to leave. "I appreciate all your help. I really mean it."

"Any time, Olivia," Jessica said earnestly.

"I'll see you in school tomorrow," Olivia said.

Jessica nodded. "Oh, and if you change your mind about looking for another dress, give me a call," she added helpfully.

Olivia watched Jessica bound down the front walk, her blond hair swinging, and shook her head. Then she went back to her room and took her dress out again, looking at it critically. *How could I possibly have thought I could wear this thing?* she thought. *Mrs. Patman would probably laugh in my face when she saw it.*

"Jessica's right," she said aloud, putting the dress back in the closet. "The Patmans are all

Roger has left now." She shook her head again, her eyes filling with tears. "If I go to the country club party with Roger, I'll make a complete fool out of us both! How in the world did I ever think the two of us could stay together?"

"Roger!" Mrs. Patman called from the patio, where she was sunning herself. "Could you come here for a moment, please?"

Roger was doing warm-up exercises on the lawn, getting ready to go for a run. "Yes, ma'am," he called, loping over to the patio.

"I've been hoping," Mrs. Patman said, setting aside the paperback she'd been holding, "that we'd have a chance to have a little private talk together, you and I. It seems," she added, taking her sunglasses off and looking directly at Roger with her icy blue eyes, "that we've *barely* had a chance to get acquainted since you've moved in."

"That's true," Roger said uneasily, stuffing his hands in the front pockets of his nylon shorts and rocking back and forth awkwardly on the balls of his feet.

"Why don't you have a seat, dear," Mrs. Patman suggested coldly. "It feels so awkward when you're just *lurching*."

Roger blushed and sat down on the wicker chair across from his aunt.

"That's better, dear," Mrs. Patman said approvingly. "Now, Roger, do you realize that I don't really know very much about what you do—away from home, that is? I don't know about your hobbies or your studies or almost *anything*. That doesn't seem right, now, does it?"

"No, ma'am," Roger said, looking down at the flagstone on the patio. "Well," he began, grinning, "I like to run."

Mrs. Patman took a handkerchief out of her bag and dabbed her forehead with it. "Yes," she said coolly. "I've been meaning to ask you about that, dear. Don't you think that running is—how shall I put this—it's not a very social sport, is it?"

"No, ma'am," Roger agreed. "I think that's why I've always liked it. Not that I don't like being social," he added hastily, "but I've always loved to be off by myself sometimes. It's a great time to think," he added shyly.

Mrs. Patman regarded him condescendingly. "Mmm," she said. "I see. And what is it you think about while you're running around, getting hot and sweaty?"

Roger laughed. "It doesn't sound very good when you put it that way," he admitted. "I don't know," he added. "I guess sometimes I think a little about the future." His face brightened as he spoke. "I think about medicine," he added.

"Medicine!" Mrs. Patman looked appalled. "Why in the world would you want to think about *that*?"

Roger smiled. "I don't think about taking it," he assured her. "But you see, I've always wanted to be a doctor."

"A doctor," she repeated.

Surely she couldn't disapprove of that, Roger thought.

"Oh, dear. I suppose it's a good profession, but it's so—so messy," she announced. "Bruce has always wanted to go into his father's business," she added approvingly.

Roger didn't have the faintest idea what to say. "Oh," Roger murmured, "that's nice."

"And what about your *friends*, Roger?" Mrs. Patman went on, picking up an emery board from the table beside her and filing her long, perfectly shaped nails. "I don't even know who your *friends* are. Why don't you tell me a little bit about them?"

"Uh, who do you mean, ma'am?" Roger asked her.

"Well, Jessica Wakefield seems like a nice girl to me. Is she a good friend of yours?"

"I guess so," Roger said uncomfortably. "I mean, no, not really. I don't know her all that well."

"Hmmm," Mrs. Patman said. "Well, what about that other little friend of yours—that girl who was here playing tennis with you and Bruce and Jessica."

"Olivia, you mean," Roger said.

"Olivia! That's it. Yes, I mean Olivia. What did you say her last name was?"

"Davidson," Roger said.

"Would I be intruding," Mrs. Patman went on, putting the emery board down and looking closely at Roger, "if I were to ask you if you plan on inviting this Olivia to be your date at our party next Saturday?"

"Yes, ma'am, I am," Roger answered. "I already asked her."

"Oh, dear," Mrs. Patman said, sighing deeply. "Roger, this may be none of my business . . . but don't you think that Olivia is a little—how shall I put it, I don't know—a little *awkward*?" Mrs. Patman asked vaguely.

"I think she's just fine," Roger said defensively. "She's the best friend I have."

"Oh, I'm sure she is," Mrs. Patman said soothingly. "But I was just thinking, Roger, that at *this* kind of party, with so many of the guests looking up to you—"

Roger waited for her to finish.

"Now, Bruce knows some lovely young ladies from the local college," Mrs. Patman told him. "I'm sure he'd be more than happy to fix you up with someone suitable. Why don't you run along and talk to him about it, dear? Bruce is always so *sure* of himself in situations like this."

Roger flushed. He didn't know what to say. He didn't want to ask Bruce for advice on anything, least of all girls. Olivia was the only girl he wanted. But his aunt looked so insistent, and the last thing Roger wanted was to make her unhappy, especially after all she'd done for him—she and Uncle Henry.

"I'll think about it," he mumbled unhappily.

"Getting a bit of sun, dear?" Henry Patman

interrupted, closing the sliding door behind him and coming out on the patio. "Hello, Roger," he boomed warmly, putting his arm around his nephew. "I've been looking for you all over the place."

"Roger and I were just getting better acquainted," Mrs. Patman said. "Isn't that right, Roger?"

"Yes, ma'am," Roger agreed.

"Well, I hope you don't mind if I steal our new nephew away for a few minutes," Mr. Patman said, his arm still around Roger. "What do you say, Rog? Would you mind giving me a hand with a few things I've got out in the garage?"

"Sure, Uncle Henry," Roger said, following his uncle down the patio steps and around the garage. His uncle grinned at him and rumpled his hair.

"It's a bit rough, isn't it, moving into a new house and having all these relatives to deal with out of the blue."

"Yes, sir," Roger mumbled. "I mean, no, sir. I mean, I'm really grateful for everything you've done for me, but sometimes I feel like everything I do is wrong."

"Don't let it get to you," Mr. Patman advised cheerfully, slamming the car trunk closed. "We're all extremely proud to have you as a member of the family, Roger. The Patman family needs someone like you."

Roger carried the packages his uncle had given him into the house, his mind reeling. He wanted so badly to make his new family proud of him, especially his uncle. He wanted so much to belong, to be one of the Patmans. But the conversation he had just had with his aunt made him feel terribly confused and upset. Why did it seem like all the things he loved weren't good enough anymore? Running was antisocial. Medicine was too messy. And Olivia . . . Olivia was awkward.

"Glad to see they're putting you to work, Rog," Bruce taunted, passing him on the stairs. Roger looked down at the boxes in his arms and glared at Bruce. Every time Bruce baited him this way he felt the way he did when he was running a race—determined not to let anything or anyone stop him. *I'm not going to let Bruce make a fool out of me anymore*, he vowed to himself. *I'm going to make the Patmans proud of me. I'm going to do things their way, no matter what I have to give up to do it!*

Ten

"Liz!" Regina whispered, excited. "I have to tell you something."

"What is it?" Elizabeth asked curiously, following Regina through the cafeteria line.

"They're ready!" Regina exclaimed. She looked around her and lowered her voice. "The photo proofs are ready. Lane just called the office. He says the magazine will be coming out any day now, and he wants me to come downtown this afternoon to see the final result."

Both Elizabeth and Regina were too engrossed in their conversation to notice that Lila Fowler had just joined them in line.

"What time do you have to meet him?" Elizabeth asked.

"He's picking me up here at two-thirty," Regina told her. "Oh, Liz, I'm so excited I could die!"

Well, well, well, Lila thought to herself, wrinkling her nose at the cheeseburger the woman behind the counter passed her. *Regina Morrow has another mysterious date in the middle of the afternoon.* She watched Elizabeth and Regina leave the cafeteria line, and a little smile came to her lips. This time maybe she'd tag along behind them! she thought. It was certainly worth missing last period to see how Regina Morrow had been spending her idle afternoons!

At two-twenty-five Lila was sitting in her lime-green Triumph, her eyes riveted on the front entrance of Sweet Valley High. Sure enough, a short while later Regina came out, looking around nervously to make sure she hadn't been noticed. *Little does she know,* Lila said to herself, chuckling slyly and turning the motor on. A minute later the beige Ferrari pulled into the parking lot. Lila watched as the handsome man jumped out of the car, ran over to Regina, and kissed her on the cheek. "I'm going to find out where those two lovebirds are nesting if it kills me," Lila said grimly.

To her surprise, the Ferrari took the main road heading downtown. *I thought they'd head some-*

where a little more secluded, Lila thought, expertly maneuvering the car so she wouldn't lose them. *Back to the scene of the first sighting!* she realized with surprise, as she saw the Ferrari pull into a parking space in front of the medical center. Lila drove past the Ferrari and found a parking spot farther up the street. She parked quickly, glancing frequently in the rearview mirror so that she wouldn't lose sight of the couple.

As she got out of her car, Lane and Regina disappeared inside the office building across the street. Lila darted after them. She could just make out a flash of Regina's blue skirt as the two disappeared into the elevator. *Time for some master sleuthing,* Lila told herself, watching the numbers above the elevator light up. At six the elevator paused for a while. *Number six it is.* Lila chuckled, pushing the up button.

Lila stepped out on the sixth floor and looked around her. Lane Townsend Agency, the letters above the big, dark, paneled door read. Lila was taken aback. She had certainly heard of the Townsend agency—everyone had—but she hadn't known the office was right here in Sweet Valley. What in the world was Regina doing there, she wondered?

There was only one way to find out, Lila decided. Taking a deep breath, she opened the heavy door.

"Can I help you?" a friendly voice inquired. The woman behind the reception desk was smiling at her cheerfully. "You haven't come to ask about the *Ingenue* competition, have you?" she went on.

Lila thought quickly. "Yes, as a matter of fact, I have," she told her. "Can you give me some information about it?"

The woman shook her head, her blond curls bouncing. "I'm afraid I really can't," she said apologetically. "Lane has been handling all the inquiries himself, and he hasn't told me much about it."

"Oh, dear," Lila said, trying to look disappointed.

"I'll tell you what," the woman said sympathetically. "Why don't I set up an appointment for you with Lane himself? He'll be able to tell you all about it."

"That would be wonderful," Lila said appreciatively. "When can I see him?"

Just then the door to the inside office opened, and a man stepped out. "Suzanne, have you seen the page proofs of *Ingenue* yet?" He shook his head, smiling. "I don't know how Lane manages to find girls like that. This Regina Morrow is a real beauty."

Lila couldn't believe her ears. Regina Morrow was appearing in *Ingenue* magazine! Did that mean she wasn't having an affair at all! Lila's head reeled. She was so stunned she hardly knew what to think. *There must be some way to convince Mr. Townsend not to print her picture,* Lila thought wildly. *He'll take one look at me,* she assured herself, *and he'll tear Regina's pictures up and start from scratch.* "When did you say I could see Mr. Townsend?" she asked the woman at the desk.

"Just a minute, Ben," Suzanne said cheerfully, turning back to Lila. "How would this Friday afternoon be?" she asked, consulting her calendar. "Four forty-five."

"That would be fine," Lila told her. Her fingers shaking, she took a card from the woman and wrote the time on it. She *had* got to stop Regina's picture from appearing in that magazine, she told herself, hurrying out of the office and pushing the down button on the elevator. She didn't know how she was going to change Lane Townsend's mind, but she had to do it!

Olivia and Roger were sitting by themselves on the front lawn after school. It was almost four o'clock, and most of the students had already disappeared.

"Did you say you had something to tell me, Liv?" Roger asked anxiously.

Olivia nodded. "I just hope you won't take it the wrong way," she said slowly.

Roger sighed. "That doesn't sound like a good beginning."

Olivia looked away from him. "Rog, I know you've been under a lot of pressure lately, and I don't want to make it harder on you. But I can't go to the party at the country club with you next weekend."

"Why not?" Roger demanded.

Olivia shook her head. "Lots of reasons," she told him. "But I guess the biggest one is that your family makes me feel really uncomfortable. I just don't think I'd be able to act myself and still have a good time."

Roger stared at her in disbelief. "Olivia, how can you possibly say that?" he demanded. "Haven't you had fun the last few times you've come over?"

Olivia sighed. "No, Roger, I haven't," she told him. "As a matter of fact, I've felt like a perfect clod."

"What are you talking about?" Roger cried.

"Look, Roger," Olivia said firmly. "You know how I feel about you, but I can't help the way I am. I guess I'm just not what the Patmans consider suitable."

"I don't see how you can say that," Roger argued. He took a deep breath. "The Patmans aren't so bad," he insisted. "You're just not giving them a chance."

"I'm sure they're not bad at all," Olivia said gently. She tried her best to smile. "In fact, I happen to be pretty crazy about one of them," she added. "But that still won't make me feel any more at ease next Saturday."

"Olivia, you have to come to that party with me!" Roger insisted.

Olivia shook her head. "I can't," she told him.

"But I've already told all of them that you're coming!" Roger cried.

Olivia jumped to her feet. This was the last straw. "Is that all you care about—being embarrassed about my backing out of a date? I thought you cared about my feelings!" she said bitterly.

"And I thought you cared about mine!" Roger said, as angry as Olivia. "If it's too much to ask you to put up with my family, maybe we should just stop seeing each other altogether!"

"I think you're absolutely right," Olivia told him. "Why don't you find someone a little better suited for your fancy new life?"

"If that's the way you're going to be about it, maybe I will," Roger replied. He couldn't believe this was Olivia talking to him. She had always been so understanding!

Olivia had run off to the bicycle rack. She bent over her bike, trying to work the lock, but her fingers were trembling so badly she couldn't do it. At last the lock gave way. Olivia jumped on the bike, her eyes blinded with tears. She had hoped that Roger would tell her she was crazy to think she didn't fit in, that he loved her and thought her behavior was perfect just the way it was. She hadn't planned on things ending up this way. "I don't care," she told herself, pedaling wildly away from the school. "I don't want to see any of those people again—not Bruce, or Jessica, and certainly not Roger!" If this was the way he wanted it, this was the way it would be!

But as she rode her bicycle down the sidewalks heading home, she couldn't help feeling sadder than she'd ever felt in her whole life.

About fifteen minutes later, Roger, turning his uncle's car up the long driveway to the Patman mansion, felt much the same way—as if, he told himself, pushing the remote-control button that opened the garage door, he'd lost his best friend.

Eleven

"Where's Jessica, Mom?" Elizabeth inquired, wandering into the Wakefields' Spanish-tiled kitchen and opening the refrigerator door.

Alice Wakefield laughed, watching her daughter's head almost disappear. "Are you interested in anything in there, or are you just browsing?" she teased.

"Interested," Elizabeth confirmed, choosing an apple and polishing it on the front of her shirt.

"Jess is out at the pool," her mother told her.

Elizabeth bit into the apple and hurried through the kitchen to the swimming pool in the backyard. Jessica was lying flat on her back on the diving board in a red string bikini, one hand

112

flung dramatically over her eyes. Elizabeth leaned over and bounced the diving board with one hand. "Look, there's a sign of life!" she exclaimed as Jessica opened one eye.

"Can't you see I'm busy, Liz?" Jessica muttered.

"Your energy level astounds me," Elizabeth said dryly. "Jess, I want to talk to you about Olivia."

"Olivia?" Jessica asked sleepily, as if she'd never heard the name before.

"Yes, Olivia," Elizabeth said firmly. "Olivia Davidson, remember? The girl you haven't let out of your sight for the past week?"

"What about her?" Jessica asked, lazily pulling herself up to a sitting position.

"Jess, I just ran into her downtown," Elizabeth told her sister, "and she looked absolutely terrible!"

"What was she wearing?" Jessica asked, looking interested at last.

Elizabeth gave her twin a dirty look. "That's *not* what I meant," she informed her. "She looked like she hasn't slept in weeks—or eaten much, for that matter. Anyway, we ended up having Cokes together, and she told me that she had a big fight with Roger the other day and they broke up."

"You're kidding," Jessica said, wide awake at last. "You mean she's not going to the party with him next Saturday?"

"I guess not," Elizabeth said. "She didn't

113

mention it, but from the way she made it sound, I don't think they'll ever even talk to each other again! Jess, I feel so sorry for her."

"So do I," Jessica said, trying her best to look sympathetic. She hopped off the diving board and grabbed the shorts and shirt she had left rolled in a ball at the side of the pool.

"Where are you going?" Elizabeth demanded.

"To offer my consolation!" Jessica called behind her, hurrying toward the back door. "It's the least I can do," she told her sister, "after Olivia and I have gotten so close."

Boy, I guess I really have misjudged Jessica this time, Elizabeth thought. *And I was beginning to think she was up to something.*

Meanwhile, Jessica was already on the phone upstairs, dialing the Patmans' number. "Roger, can I come over for a few minutes?" Jessica asked when he answered. "I've got to talk to you."

After all, she hadn't told Elizabeth who she was going to console, she said to herself, quickly changing her clothes. The party at the country club was only a week away, she thought. She had no time to lose.

"Why, Jessica Wakefield, what a nice surprise!" Mrs. Patman exclaimed. "Have you come over to see Roger?"

"As a matter of fact, I have," Jessica said politely.

"Please come in," Mrs. Patman urged.

"Roger's out on the patio, reading. I'll take you out to him, dear."

Jessica followed Mrs. Patman through the immense, high-ceilinged foyer. She was already imagining the fabulous parties she and Roger could have in the Patman mansion.

"Here he is," Mrs. Patman said, opening the glass doors onto the huge patio. "Roger, look who's come over to visit you. Jessica Wakefield!"

"Hi, Jess," Roger said, setting his novel down beside him.

"I'll just leave you two alone," Mrs. Patman said happily, closing the glass doors behind her.

"Roger, Liz told me that you and Olivia had a big fight," Jessica said, getting right to the point.

"She did?" Roger demanded. "Where did she see Olivia?" His face brightened at the mention of Olivia's name.

This won't do at all, Jessica thought. "That doesn't really matter," she said firmly. "I just wanted to let you know how sorry I am, Roger."

"Thanks, Jess," Roger said dully.

"But I guess it was kind of inevitable, wasn't it?" Jessica said brightly, plopping down on the lounge chair across from Roger. "After all, you and Olivia are so completely different from each other."

"What do you mean?" Roger demanded.

Jessica shrugged. "It was one thing before, when you were kind of quiet," she pointed out. "But it seems to me that you've gotten so much

115

friendlier these days. You're probably too outgoing for Olivia now. She's so shy."

"I hadn't thought of it that way before," Roger said, looking at Jessica with interest.

"I probably shouldn't tell you this," Jessica said coyly, "but Olivia told me that she's jealous of you, now that you're living with the Patmans. I just don't think she can stand the fact that you're so wealthy now, Roger. In fact, Olivia told me she was going to break her date to the dance with you so you'd turn up by yourself and everyone would laugh at you."

Roger's face went completely red. "I can't believe Olivia would do something like that."

Jessica sighed. "I know," she admitted. "It's pretty hard to understand what's gotten into her these days."

"Who does she think she is," Roger said furiously. "Didn't she think I could ask someone else to the dance?"

"Well, that's what I told her," Jessica said smoothly. "I told her you'd be able to go with anyone you wanted at the drop of a hat." Jessica looked down at her hands, smiling a little, as if she were embarrassed. "Which sounded kind of funny coming from me," she admitted.

"Why?" Roger asked.

Jessica flushed. "Well, *I* still don't have a date to your party myself," she admitted.

"Jessica!" Roger exclaimed, his face lighting up as if a brilliant idea had just occurred to him.

116

"How would you like to come to the party with me?"

Jessica pretended to look completely confused. "You mean come as your date?" she asked doubtfully.

"Why not?" Roger demanded. "Come on, Jess!"

Jessica smiled softly as she pretended to think it over. "But what about Olivia?" she asked.

"Forget about her," Roger said. *Aunt Marie was right about Olivia all along*, he thought to himself. *I wish I'd listened to her sooner*.

"Roger, I'd love to go with you," Jessica said.

"Then it's a date!" Roger cried. "I'm so glad I thought of it," he told her, grinning.

"So am I," Jessica murmured. *You can't possibly know how glad*, she thought to herself, a little smile of satisfaction on her lips.

"What did Jessica want?" Mrs. Patman asked, joining Roger in the breakfast room after he'd shown his guest out to her car.

Roger thought for a minute and then shook his head, cutting in half the sandwich he had fixed himself. He might as well tell his aunt the truth—it would make life in his new home a lot easier.

"Jessica and I have decided to go to the party together," he said, taking a big bite of his sandwich.

"Why, Roger, what a wonderful idea!" Mrs.

117

Patman exclaimed. "But what happened to that little friend of yours, the one you were so keen on before?"

"Olivia," Roger said firmly, "doesn't seem to want to go with me anymore. We had a big fight," he added.

"Miranda, pour Roger a glass of milk," Mrs. Patman called to the servant, who was putting groceries into the refrigerator. "Don't you worry, dear," she told Roger. "You and Jessica will make such a beautiful couple!"

"Yeah, I guess so," Roger said, taking a gulp of the cold milk Miranda handed him. *But I don't want to be a "beautiful couple,"* an unhappy little voice inside of him said sadly. *I want to be with Olivia.*

"Lila Fowler? Oh, yes, Mr. Townsend is expecting you," Suzanne said, checking the calendar on her desk. "Why don't you just have a seat?" she suggested. "I'll let him know you're here."

"Lane," she said into the phone on her desk. "Miss Fowler is here to see you."

Lila twisted nervously on the hard chair. She hoped she looked all right. The night before, she had set her hair on long rollers, and in the morning she had sprayed it with hair spray to keep the curls in. Her face felt a little stiff from all the makeup she'd put on that afternoon, but she was sure the total effect was glamorous. *Regina doesn't even wear makeup,* she thought scornfully. Lila was wearing one of her most expensive outfits—a pair of cream-colored linen trousers, high heels, and a turquoise silk blouse with a bow.

"You must be Lila," Lane Townsend said, coming forward with a smile. He put his hand out, and Lila shook it awkwardly. Lane took a closer look at the girl, and his expression grew puzzled. "You look familiar," he told her. "Have I seen you in here before?"

"No, sir," Lila said, hoping he wouldn't remember seeing her at Sweet Valley High.

"Hmm," Lane said, smiling. "I see so many pretty girls," he told her. "You'll have to forgive me. I'm pleased to meet you now, anyway. Why don't you come inside?"

Lila marveled at the luxurious offices behind the reception area. The walls were mirrored, and the creamy carpeting sank beneath her high heels. "Why don't you have a seat in here?" Lane said kindly, leading Lila into an immense, wood-paneled room with a huge desk at one end. The walls were covered with pictures of famous models, most of them with their arms around celebrities. Lila took a deep breath and sat down on the chair Lane was pointing to.

"Now," he said, sinking into the chair behind the desk and lighting a pipe, "what can I do for you?"

Lila blushed. "Well, sir, I wanted to learn more about the *Ingenue* competition."

Lane sighed. "Oh, dear. Our competition ended weeks ago."

Lila looked at Lane in dismay.

He stood up and walked over to the window. "As a matter of fact, we made a real discovery for that spot," he told her. "I happened to run into a girl, not much older than you, I'd guess, when I was downtown one day. This doesn't often happen to agents, Lila," he said kindly, "but when it does, it makes the whole business worthwhile. The girl's name is Regina, and she's absolutely perfect." He shook his head, smiling, and drew on his pipe. "In fact, she's so perfect we decided to take her on the spot, and we cut the competition short."

"I see," Lila said shortly, her face burning.

"She's a pretty unusual girl," Lane went on thoughtfully, not noticing the expression on Lila's face. "Not only is she beautiful, and absolutely unspoiled as far as appearance goes—but it turns out that's she's managed to overcome a real handicap and live a normal life. More than normal, in fact. *Ingenue* was so impressed that they decided to use her on the cover of this month's issue and run a full feature story about her inside."

"How nice," Lila said flatly. The last thing she wanted was to hear somebody telling her how wonderful Regina Morrow was. Lane Townsend *must* be in love with her, she thought meanly. Wasn't that how a lot of models and actresses got their start?

As if he'd read her mind, Lane stood up and smiled at her. "The real thanks, as usual, goes to my wife, Laurie. She's the editor of *Ingenue*, and she's the one who spotted Regina when we were downtown together."

"Well, thank you very much for taking the time to see me," Lila mumbled, reaching for her purse. She'd heard more than enough.

Lane laughed. "It's my business to meet pretty girls," he told her. "Lila, try not to be too disappointed about the modeling job. You're a pretty girl, but you don't really have the right facial structure, I'm afraid. You wouldn't like how flat your face would look in photographs. Anyway," he told her, seeing her to the door, "modeling is hard work. You'll probably thank me a few years from now."

I bet I will, Lila thought bitterly, running out of his office and almost tripping on the thick carpeting in her high heels. *Flat face indeed!* She raced past Suzanne and punched the down button on the elevator with a trembling finger. "Beautiful afternoon," the man in the lobby remarked, but Lila didn't answer. "It's a *horrible* afternoon," she muttered, dashing outside and hurrying to her car. It struck Lila that life in Sweet Valley had been a lot *lovelier* before Regina Morrow moved in.

Twelve

The afternoon of the party, Roger was in Mr. Patman's dressing room, looking in his uncle's armoire for a pair of cuff links. "Where in the world does he keep those things?" he muttered, opening yet another drawer and scratching his head.

Suddenly he heard a rustling in the master bedroom. Mrs. Patman had come in and was dialing a number on the phone. "Marjorie?" she said into the receiver. "It's Marie Patman. How *are* you, dear?"

Roger froze, the drawer of the armoire still open. He didn't know what to do. If he came out of the bedroom right away, his aunt might be angry at him for going through his uncle's drawers alone. His uncle Henry had given him permission that morning to look for cuff links, but Roger was still afraid of getting on his aunt's bad side—especially since things had gone so beautifully all week. He decided to keep really quiet and just wait until she had hung up the phone and gone back downstairs.

"I just wanted to make sure you and Humphrey could make it to the party tonight," he heard her say into the phone. "Yes, we're looking forward to it, too," she went on. "I think it will be a really *special* evening." There was a long pause, and Roger held his breath, trying to stay perfectly still. "Oh, no, thank heavens!" Mrs. Patman said, laughing. "He's through with her. And I can't say I'm sorry, either. She was pretty dreadful."

Roger froze. *Who is Aunt Marie talking about? It had better not be Olivia*, he thought, his face getting hot.

"Oh, *yes*, dear," Mrs. Patman said assuringly. "He's going with Jessica Wakefield. Do you remember her from the barbecue?" There was another pause, and Mrs. Patman continued. "That's right. The pretty blonde with the twin sister. As a matter of fact, I think Jessica's the one I really have to be grateful to." She chuckled.

Roger stood perfectly still, his mouth dry and his heart pounding. What in the world was going on?

"Well," Mrs. Patman confided, her voice

dropping, "I don't know *how* Jessica did it, exactly. She and I had a chat the day of the barbecue, and I pointed out how entirely unsuitable I thought Roger's little friend was. Jessica seemed to understand me pretty well. The next thing I knew she was taking the girl with her everywhere. And a week ago Roger told me he was through with her!" She listened to her friend on the other end, then laughed.

"That's right, Marjorie," she agreed. "They're learning younger all the time. Well, dear, I've got to run downstairs and have a word with the caterers. I'm *so* glad you and Humphrey can still come this evening."

Roger waited until he heard the click of the receiver and the swish of his aunt's dress as she moved across the room. The door closed softly behind her, and he burst out of the dressing room, his uncle's cuff links completely forgotten.

Roger had never been so angry in his life. Now that he knew the truth, the events of the last few weeks seemed to make much more sense. So that was why Jessica had suddenly been so friendly to Olivia! He slammed the door to the master bedroom and ran down the hall to his own room.

He couldn't believe he had listened to all the nonsense Jessica had fed him about Olivia's being jealous of him. Even worse, he had allowed himself to be part of a setup because he hadn't been able to stick up for himself and tell his aunt to mind her own business. He had become so caught up in being a Patman that he'd actually begun to believe that Olivia was wrong for him. "No wonder she never wants to see me again!" he cried aloud.

Roger caught sight of the tuxedo his uncle had laid out for him on his bed, and he felt like crying. *There's no way I'm taking Jessica to the dance tonight*, he vowed silently. His first thought was that he wouldn't go at all. But it occurred to him that not going wouldn't really accomplish anything.

Roger picked up the telephone receiver, a plan beginning to form as he dialed the Wakefields' number. The phone rang once in the Wakefield house, then twice. What really mattered, he thought, was making Olivia understand the truth, even if she'd never forgive him. "Answer," he whispered into the phone, his face flushed with anger and anxiety. He just hoped he wasn't too late.

"Telephone, Jessica!" Alice Wakefield called, coming to the foot of the stairs. "How many times do I have to ask you girls to get the phone when you hear it?" she scolded. Mrs. Wakefield was hard at work on a new design, and she hated to be interrupted when she was in the middle of a project.

"Sorry, Mom," Jessica said. "I was trying to get this lemon rinse out of my hair. I've got it," she added, picking up the telephone in her bedroom.

"Hi, Roger!" she exclaimed, rubbing her damp hair with a towel. "What's up?"

"Jessica, can I come over for a few minutes?" Roger asked. "I need your advice." He was trying as hard as he could to make his voice sound natural.

"Uh—sure, Rog," Jessica answered. "Is anything wrong?"

"No, Jess, not a thing," Roger lied. "Hey, is Liz going to be around, too?"

"I think so," Jessica said, more puzzled by the minute. "Why?"

"I'd like to talk to the two of you together. Can I come over right away?"

"Sure," Jessica said, hanging the receiver up and combing her hair thoughtfully. Roger had sounded really strange, she thought. She hoped nothing had gone wrong.

Half an hour later Roger was sitting by the Wakefield pool.

"What's going on, Roger?" Elizabeth asked, her blue-green eyes warm with concern. A few minutes earlier she'd gotten home from the library, where she'd been doing research for the playwrights' competition. After several days of thought, she'd decided to write about her favorite poet, Elizabeth Barrett Browning.

Roger stood up and paced before the twins, his hands jammed in his pockets. "I need your help," he told them, looking from one twin to

126

the other. "I've made a terrible mistake, and unless I do something right away I'll never forgive myself! As it is," he added, "Olivia may never forgive me."

Jessica bit her lip and tried to keep her face composed.

"Tell us what's wrong, Roger," Elizabeth suggested, her voice low and understanding.

"Jess, I just can't go to the dance with you tonight!" Roger burst out. "How can I go with you and have a wonderful time when Olivia's home by herself, hating me?"

"I don't know," Jessica said shortly. Elizabeth shot her twin a quick look.

"What can we do to help, Roger?" she asked quietly.

Roger pretended to think it over. "I wonder . . ." he began. "No, that would never work," he told himself, shaking his head.

"What wouldn't work?" Elizabeth prompted.

"Well, I was just thinking that if all three of us went over to Olivia's right now, we might be able to persuade her to change her mind. Jess, I know how *close* you and Olivia have become," Roger said pointedly.

Jessica chewed her lip anxiously. From the way he was looking at her, she realized that Roger knew a lot more than that. "I think you and Liz should go without me," she told him. "Liz is a lot better than I am at things like this. She's a real diplomat."

"Thanks," Elizabeth said dryly. Maybe Jessica

hadn't been helping Olivia all along. She looked hard at her twin. "It wouldn't be *awkward* for you for some reason, would it, Jess?"

"Come on, Liz," Roger urged her. "We don't have much time!"

Jessica watched her sister and Roger hurry to his car and shook her head in disbelief. She couldn't believe she had just been stood up for the biggest party of the season—and by the guest of honor himself! She had been looking forward to the party for *ages*, and now everyone would know that Roger had dumped her.

But Jessica Wakefield rarely brooded for long. She got up and headed into the family room, where she picked up the phone. One thing was for certain—Jessica wasn't going to sit home alone that night feeling sorry for herself.

"Hello?" a male voice answered.

"Neil Freemount!" Jessica exclaimed, her face brightening a little already. "This just may be your lucky day. How would you like to take me to the Patmans' party at the country club tonight?"

Thirteen

"Liz, do you think she'll even let me inside?" Roger asked, turning his car onto Olivia's street.

"I don't see why not, Roger," Elizabeth assured him. But privately, she had her doubts. Roger had told her the whole story, and it all made sense. *Leave it to Jessica*, Elizabeth thought.

"Well, here goes nothing," Roger said nervously, pulling his car into the Davidsons' driveway. He sat perfectly still for a minute, looking with pleasure at the ranch house in front of him. The Davidsons' house was small but very pretty, the flat, red-tiled Spanish roof complementing the white stucco facade. Then Roger and Elizabeth got out of the car and walked up the flagstone walk to the front door. Taking a deep breath, Roger rang the bell.

"Why, hello, Roger," Mrs. Davidson said cheerfully. "I haven't seen you for a long time. How have you been?"

"I've been all right," Roger told her, wondering how much Olivia had told her mother about him. "Do you know Elizabeth Wakefield?"

"I've certainly heard a lot about you," Mrs. Davidson said, smiling at Elizabeth. "You write the 'Eyes and Ears' column."

"Yes, I do," Elizabeth said, smiling back.

"Why don't you two come into the garden?" Mrs. Davidson suggested. "I'll see what Olivia is up to."

"This is beautiful!" Elizabeth gasped, as Olivia's mother led them into a large, rectangular garden that formed the center of the Davidsons' house. The garden was closed over with a glass ceiling, and at its center was a marble fountain surrounded by plants and flowers. Mrs. Davidson smiled. "My brother is an architect," she told her guests, "and he designed this house for us when Olivia was born."

A few minutes later she came back, looking with some confusion from Roger to Elizabeth. "Olivia said she'll be out in a few minutes," she told them. "Can I bring you a cold drink while you're waiting?"

"No, thank you," the two said in unison, smiling nervously at each other.

Olivia finally entered the garden room, and

Elizabeth thought her friend had never looked prettier. Her brown curls were held back by a silver-and-gold braided rope, and she was wearing a loose, man-sized cotton shirt belted over a flowered skirt. She was barefoot, but she held her head so high that she looked—like a princess, Elizabeth thought for the second time.

"Hi, Liz," Olivia said shyly, smiling with apparent effort. She turned to Roger, and the smile faded, but her voice stayed perfectly calm. "Hi, Roger," she added. Olivia assured herself that neither of them could tell how upset she had been when she'd seen Roger's car pulling into the driveway ten minutes earlier. She had been writing furiously in her journal, her eyes welling up with tears as she imagined Roger and Jessica dancing in each other's arms. But now she was perfectly composed—at least, on the surface.

"Olivia," Roger began, "I owe you a big apology."

Olivia stared at him. This was the last thing she'd expected Roger to say! "What do you mean?" she asked tentatively.

"I've made a real fool out of myself these past couple of weeks," Roger continued, shaking his head. "Liv, I have so much to explain to you! Will you hear me out?"

Olivia looked from Roger to Elizabeth. "What's going on?" she demanded. "Where's Jessica?"

Elizabeth flushed. However badly her twin behaved, she hated to speak ill of her to anyone else. In fact, Elizabeth usually ended up defending Jessica. But this time anger got the better of her. "Jess is at home, Olivia," she told the girl. "She's caused enough trouble lately!"

"Maybe I'd better sit down," Olivia said weakly, pulling a chair over to where her guests were sitting. "OK. Now what in the world are you two talking about?"

"Olivia, I overheard my aunt on the phone this morning," Roger began. She looked at him quizzically, and his face turned red. "I didn't mean to eavesdrop," he said hurriedly. "It was an accident. She was talking to Mrs. Ferguson, that terrible woman I told you about who I dumped wine on that night at dinner. Well, my aunt told Mrs. Ferguson this morning that she and Jessica had had a little talk a few weeks ago at our barbecue and the two of them decided to go to work on both of us. The plan," he added bitterly, "was to make you feel uncomfortable being around me and to make me feel that you weren't good enough for the Patmans."

Olivia blushed hotly. "You mean all that time Jessica was inviting me to go places with her she was really trying to make me feel like a misfit?" she asked. She shook her head. "Well, it sure worked," she added.

Elizabeth felt terrible; she didn't know what to say. Roger spoke up, "It wasn't all Jessica's fault. If I hadn't been so insecure about being a Patman, I would never have fallen for her little game. But I just wasn't confident enough to stand up to my aunt. She disapproves of all the things that really matter to me. She wants me to take up tennis instead of running, and get interested in business instead of medicine. She wants me to be just like Bruce. And I'm not. But I didn't have the courage to let her know who I really am, and I was too worried about pleasing her to see through her little plan. In fact I fell for it completely."

Olivia looked thoughtful. "You have a point," she told Roger. "But you're not the only one to blame." She laughed ruefully, remembering how mortified she'd been at the barbecue and on the tennis courts. "If I hadn't been so insecure about myself, nothing Jessica said or did would have fazed me in the least." She laughed again. "Wow, we've really acted like a pair of prize idiots," she declared.

"Olivia," Roger said, "the first thing I thought when I heard my aunt this morning was that I wouldn't go to that party tonight if they paid me. But then I thought about it again. The Patmans are having this party tonight to make an impression, and there's one impression I'd really like to make. Olivia, will you come to the party with me?"

Olivia stared at him. "I don't understand," she said. "You still want to go with me, even after you know how your aunt feels?"

Roger nodded. "I want to show them that being part of the Patman family may change my name and the amount of money I have, but it's not going to change *me*," Roger declared. "I love you, Olivia, and nothing's going to stop me from seeing you—not tonight and not in the future. And I want everyone to see that, especially my aunt—that is, if you'll come with me," he added, looking anxious.

"I'm still not going to be right for the Patmans," Olivia warned him.

"You're right for *one* Patman," Roger told her, reaching out and taking her hand. "In fact, you're perfect. And I happen to think that between the two of us we can make the rest of the bunch realize that that's all that matters!"

"Well . . ." Olivia said uncertainly, looking from one expectant face to the other. Then she burst out laughing. For the first time in weeks, Olivia felt like herself again. "OK!" she cried. "You're on, Roger Patman!"

"It's almost five o'clock!" Elizabeth exclaimed, looking at her watch and jumping up. "We'd better get going, or none of us is going to make it tonight!"

"The girl's got a point." Roger grinned. He stood, took Olivia's hands in his, and pulled her up and into his arms. "I'll be back to pick you up in a couple of hours," he whispered to her. "Olivia, you've made me happier than I've ever been!"

"Liz," Olivia said anxiously as she was showing her two guests to the door, "will you come to my bedroom for a minute? There's something I want to ask you."

Elizabeth followed Olivia to her bedroom and stood waiting as Olivia rummaged through her closet. "Now, tell me the truth, Liz," she insisted, taking out the lilac-colored dress she had labored over. "What do you think of this? Am I going to be the laughingstock of the whole party and embarrass Roger if I wear it?"

Elizabeth ran her hand over the fine cotton, her eyes widening. "This isn't the dress you made, is it?" she asked.

Olivia nodded. "Tell me the truth, Liz. Is it terrible?"

"Terrible?" Elizabeth stared at Olivia and then burst out laughing. "Liv, this is absolutely gorgeous," she told her. "I can't believe you actually made this!"

Olivia looked as if the question she were about to ask embarrassed her deeply. "Elizabeth," she said seriously, "do you think I'll make Roger feel uncomfortable if I wear it? It won't be like anyone else's, you know. I just don't want to hurt him."

Elizabeth shook her head. "Liv, don't you understand that Roger loves you because you *are* different? Of course no one else will have a dress like yours! It's perfectly beautiful, and I think Roger will be as proud of you in it as he could possibly be!" Impulsively Elizabeth gave Olivia a quick hug. "I'm pretty proud of you, too," she said, laughing.

Olivia laughed, too. "I feel sort of like Cinderella," she said happily, putting the dress back in her closet.

"So do I," Elizabeth cried, looking at her watch. "I'm going to turn into a pumpkin if I'm not home in ten minutes! Go take a long bath," she advised her friend, "and then put on that gorgeous dress. I have a feeling this is going to be some party!"

"Jessica Wakefield!" Elizabeth yelled, banging on the bathroom door over the noise of the shower, where Jessica was singing at top volume. Elizabeth rattled the doorknob furiously. "I'm coming in!" she threatened.

The singing stopped, and a second later Jessica opened the door so suddenly that Elizabeth almost fell on her.

"Liz!" Jessica cried, tightening the bright-blue towel that was wrapped around her. "I've been waiting for you to get home for *ages*!"

"Oh, have you really?" Elizabeth fumed, stomping behind her sister into her bedroom and slamming her door behind them.

"You'd better start getting ready," Jessica told her. "You don't want to be late for the dance, do you?"

"The *dance*," Elizabeth said angrily, "is exactly what I want to talk to you about, Jess."

"The *dance*," Jessica mimicked her twin, "will just have to wait a minute, Elizabeth Wakefield. Did you know anything about this?" she demanded, holding up the brand-new issue of *Ingenue* magazine.

Elizabeth gasped. "Where did you get that?" she demanded, yanking it out of her sister's damp hand. Sure enough, Regina Morrow was on the cover, looking more beautiful than Elizabeth could ever have imagined.

"Cara brought it over," Jessica told her. "She got it at the drugstore in the mall. And what I want to know," she said, rubbing her damp hair with a towel, "is why you don't look one bit surprised, Elizabeth Wakefield."

Elizabeth sank onto Jessica's bed, pushing aside the mounds of clothing. "Wait just one minute, little sister," she said, referring to the fact that she was four minutes older than Jessica. "We're going to take all this one step at a time. And the first thing I want to know is exactly what you thought you were doing to Olivia Davidson these past few weeks."

Jessica stared at her, her blue-green eyes wide with innocence. "I was just trying to help, Liz," she said sweetly.

"Trying to help with *what*?" Elizabeth demanded. "Trying to make Olivia feel like she wasn't good enough for Roger?"

"Liz, you know I never would have done something like that on purpose," Jessica insisted. "How was I supposed to know Olivia was so insecure? I really did want to help her," she said. "But somehow I just seemed to do everything wrong."

"You sure did," Elizabeth told her.

As if she sensed her twin was softening, Jessica flung her arms around Elizabeth in a damp embrace. "Liz, you know I didn't mean to hurt Roger or Olivia, don't you?" she demanded.

Elizabeth shook her head.

"I'd never do anything so hurtful," Jessica assured her. "Take Lila Fowler, for instance. You know, Liz, I never believed a word of that gossip she was spreading about Regina. Do you know who that older man is that Regina was supposedly seeing?"

"Who?" Elizabeth asked weakly.

Jessica thumbed through the new issue of *Ingenue*, opening it to the article on Regina. "It was Lane Townsend, the head of the Lane Townsend Agency!" she exclaimed. "Regina looks pretty good, don't you think?"

"She looks gorgeous," Elizabeth agreed, looking at the magazine over her twin's shoulder.

"Liz, tell me the truth," Jessica said, standing up and sucking her cheeks in experimentally. "How do you think I'd look as a cover girl?"

"Jessica Wakefield, don't even give it a thought!" Elizabeth burst out. She couldn't help laughing at her twin's expression. It was impossible to stay angry with Jessica, however hard she tried.

"So I take it you found another date for the dance tonight," Elizabeth added, heading for the door with the magazine tucked under her arm.

"I'm going with Neil," Jessica said airily,

opening a dresser drawer and frowning at its contents. "Oh, Liz—speaking of dates, I almost forgot to tell you. Todd called three times while you were out. He said he absolutely *has* to talk to you. I think it had something to do with Regina and the magazine," she added.

Oh, no, Elizabeth thought, closing Jessica's door and heading for the bathroom. *This sure is going to be some evening!*

Fourteen

"Doesn't the club look wonderful?" Neil asked Jessica. The stately columns in front of the main building glowed from the floodlights on the lawn. Jessica shivered, not from cold but from excitement.

"Are you chilly?" Neil asked, taking the opportunity to put his arms around her.

Jessica shook her head, her eyes sparkling. It was a beautiful evening. "Let's stay out here for a minute," she begged. From this vantage point they could watch cars pulling up and couples alighting. Besides, Jessica loved to make an entrance, and she knew she looked fabulous. She was wearing a creamy dress with a deep neckline, and her gold lavaliere glinted against her tanned skin.

"I thought Elizabeth and Todd were following us," Neil said. "Where do you suppose they are?"

"Oh, I don't know," Jessica said, shrugging. "I think Todd wanted to talk to Liz about something. Look, here comes Lila. Do you know who that is she's with?"

Neil shook his head, taking a good look at the boy who was gallantly offering Lila his arm.

"It must be that college guy she's been raving about," Jessica mused. "I think his name is Drake."

"Come on, Jess, let's go inside," Neil urged.

The ballroom was located in the main building of the country club. Even Jessica, who was a bit sour on the Patmans right now, had to admit it looked beautiful. The tables lining either side of the room were covered with snowy lace tablecloths. Each had a centerpiece on it, a large, clear glass bowl of water with tiny candles floating on top. The air was rich with the perfume of flowers. They were all over the room—on the tables and in huge arrangements near the windows and doors. By the time Jessica and Neil came through the main entrance, the dance floor was already crowded with familiar faces. A live band was playing from a raised dais on one side of the ballroom, a four-piece combo from one of the best jazz clubs downtown. "They've sure gone all out," Neil whispered.

"Why, Jessica, how nice to see you," Mrs. Patman said, taking Jessica's hand as she stepped in front of the receiving line. Mrs. Patman looked absolutely splendid. Her black hair was piled high on her head, and the round neckline of her deep-blue satin dress set off the diamond necklace she was wearing.

"I'm so happy to be here tonight," Jessica said politely. If Mrs. Patman was surprised to see her there with Neil, she didn't show it.

"Jessica!" Roger exclaimed, taking her hand with mock courtesy. "I thought you'd be far too tired to be able to come tonight. Didn't you think so, Liv?" he inquired, turning toward Olivia. "After all she's done for you in the last couple of weeks?"

"I'm feeling surprisingly well," Jessica said.

"And I see that Neil's the lucky man!" Roger went on, turning to Neil.

"What was that all about?" Neil demanded as they moved toward the dance floor.

"I haven't the faintest idea," Jessica said, slipping into his arms as the music began. "I think Roger's newfound wealth must be making him a little dizzy." She giggled.

"Hey, your sister finally made it," Neil pointed out, looking across the dance floor as Elizabeth and Todd came into the ballroom.

"Isn't this beautiful?" Elizabeth said, taking Todd's arm as they moved through the receiving line. Elizabeth greeted each of the Patmans politely, but when she came to Olivia, she gave the girl a hug. "You look beautiful," she said warmly, and meant it. The lilac-colored fabric of Olivia's dress was a perfect complement to her fair complexion and brown curls. And no amount of money or preparation could have produced the flush of color in Olivia's cheeks or the sparkle in her eyes. She looked radiant, Elizabeth thought. She had never seen Olivia so happy.

The musicians started a slow song, and Todd's voice got husky. "Let's dance," he said, drawing Elizabeth into his arms.

"Does that mean you're not mad at me anymore?" Elizabeth teased him, encircling his neck with her arms. "I thought you were going to make me walk here after you saw Regina's picture on the magazine cover!"

"I was a little hurt," Todd admitted, putting his mouth against Elizabeth's ear. "I didn't like the thought of you holding out on me. But you know, Liz, that's one of the things I like best about you. You're a good friend, and you can keep a promise."

"Well, what should I promise next?" Elizabeth murmured, tightening her arms around him.

"Just promise to have a good time tonight," Todd said softly. "That's all I ask."

I can hardly say no to that, Elizabeth thought, leaning against Todd and closing her eyes. After all her anxiety, it looked as if this dance was going to be one of the nicest she'd ever been to.

* * *

"Who's this?" Olivia asked Roger under her breath. She was relieved to see the last of the guests coming through the receiving line. She had never before smiled so much in a single hour—though she had to admit it wasn't all that hard, not with Roger beside her.

Roger looked at the couple coming toward them and grimaced. "Marjorie and Humphrey Ferguson," he told her. "Those who know them well call them 'The Bad and the Ugly.' "

"Why, Roger!" Mrs. Ferguson exclaimed, stopping short and looking at Olivia as if she were a bug. "What a surprise! I thought that pretty blond girl was going to be your date this evening!"

The receiving line went dead quiet, and Olivia turned red right to the roots of her hair. Roger cleared his throat.

"Mrs. Ferguson, this is my girlfriend, Olivia Davidson," he said firmly. "There was a little misunderstanding earlier, and luckily Olivia was able to come after all. I'm very pleased to introduce her to you."

"Well!" Mrs. Ferguson said. She made a high nasal noise and put her nose in the air. "How nice to meet you," she said to Olivia, looking as if anything in the whole world would be nicer. Roger and Olivia looked at each other and grinned.

"Roger," Mrs. Patman said as the receiving line broke up, "could I have a word with you for a moment?"

"No," Cara said, not looking very interested. "Who is he?"

"Who *is* he?" Lila repeated. "You tell her, Caroline."

"He's wonderful," Caroline began, looking from Lila to Cara. "He lives in Cold Springs. That's why he couldn't make it tonight," she explained. "He couldn't get away this weekend."

Cara looked more interested. "Is she serious, Lila?" she demanded.

"Of course I'm serious!" Caroline said hotly. "I got a letter from him just this morning," she added.

Lila laughed. "Another one of her famous letters." Out of the corner of her eye she noticed that Regina had gone back out to the dance floor. *Good riddance*, Lila thought.

"Can I read it?" Cara asked. It was clear that she was having as hard a time believing Caroline Pearce had a boyfriend as Jessica and Lila had. It wasn't that Caroline was unattractive; it was that her personality was so unpleasant that very few people liked her.

"Here it is," Caroline said, rummaging through her bag and coming up with an open envelope.

"She *is* serious," Cara said in amazement, taking the letter from Caroline.

" 'My dearest Caroline,' " she read, beginning to attract attention. Several other girls came closer to listen to Adam's letter.

"How I wish I could be with you tonight at the dance. But, Caroline, as long as you know I love you, everything will be all right. You asked me the other day how much I loved you. Caroline, it's pretty hard to measure how I feel. Let me put it this way: I love you to the depth and breadth and height my soul can reach when feeling out of sight. And if you'll be mine, nothing shall ever keep us apart. I'll love you even more after our deaths."

"Ugh," Cara said, putting the letter down. "He sounds kind of morbid. Why is he going to love you more when you're dead?"

"That's an *expression*, silly," Lila said, grabbing the letter. "This guy sure is poetic," she told Caroline. She scanned the last line or two quickly and shook her head. " 'Out of sight' is a good description," she smirked. "And what's all this about nothing keeping you two apart? It sounds like something kept you apart tonight."

Caroline blushed hotly. "He meant our *souls*," she told them, taking the letter back and putting it into her purse.

"So when do we get to meet this guy?" Lila demanded. "He can't stay up in Cold Springs forever."

"Yeah, Caroline, invite him down," Cara urged, laughing. "He can help me with my English paper next week!"

150

"As a matter of fact, he *is* coming down," Caroline said defensively.

Cara and Lila exchanged glances. "When?" they asked, almost in unison.

"I'm not sure," Caroline answered. "Maybe next weekend. He's going to see if he can get the car."

"Maybe his soul can just sort of float over from Cold Springs," Cara said, giggling. She and Lila opened the door of the lounge and walked back onto the dance floor, and Caroline walked slowly over to the mirror.

She sighed, remembering the sound of Lila and Cara's laughter. Elizabeth had just come into the ladies' lounge, and she stopped short when she saw the strange expression on Caroline's face.

"Caroline, are you OK?" she asked.

Caroline nodded. "I'm fine, Elizabeth," she said weakly. But actually Caroline didn't feel fine at all.

This is going to be a long evening, she thought to herself. *And something tells me that the week ahead won't be easy, either.*

What is Caroline afraid of? Find out in Sweet Valley High #17, LOVE LETTERS.

☐	26741	**DOUBLE LOVE #1**	$2.75
☐	26621	**SECRETS #2**	$2.75
☐	26627	**PLAYING WITH FIRE #3**	$2.75
☐	26746	**POWER PLAY #4**	$2.75
☐	26742	**ALL NIGHT LONG #5**	$2.75
☐	26813	**DANGEROUS LOVE #6**	$2.75
☐	26622	**DEAR SISTER #7**	$2.75
☐	26744	**HEARTBREAKER #8**	$2.75
☐	26626	**RACING HEARTS #9**	$2.75
☐	26620	**WRONG KIND OF GIRL #10**	$2.75
☐	26824	**TOO GOOD TO BE TRUE #11**	$2.75
☐	26688	**WHEN LOVE DIES #12**	$2.75
☐	26619	**KIDNAPPED #13**	$2.75
☐	26764	**DECEPTIONS #14**	$2.75
☐	26765	**PROMISES #15**	$2.75
☐	26740	**RAGS TO RICHES #16**	$2.75
☐	24723	**LOVE LETTERS #17**	$2.50
☐	26687	**HEAD OVER HEELS #18**	$2.75
☐	26823	**SHOWDOWN #19**	$2.75
☐	24947	**CRASH LANDING! #20**	$2.50

Prices and availability subject to change without notice.

Buy them at your local bookstore or use this convenient coupon for ordering:

Bantam Books, Inc., Dept. SVH, 414 East Golf Road, Des Plaines, Ill. 60016

Please send me the books I have checked above. I am enclosing $_____
(please add $1.50 to cover postage and handling). Send check or money order
—no cash or C.O.D.'s please.

Mr/Mrs/Miss _____

Address _____

City _____ State/Zip _____

SVH—4/87

Please allow four to six weeks for delivery. This offer expires 10/87.

SWEET DREAMS are fresh, fun and exciting—alive with the flavor of the contemporary teen scene—the joy and doubt of *first love*. If you've missed any SWEET DREAMS titles, from #1 to #100, then you're missing out on *your* kind of stories, written about people like *you*!

☐	26843	KISS & TELL #92 Janet Quin-Harkin	$2.50
☐	26743	THE GREAT BOY CHASE #93 Janet Quin-Harkin	$2.50
☐	25132	SECOND CHANCES #94 Nany Levinso	$2.25
☐	25178	NO STRINGS ATTACHED #95 Eileen Hehl	$2.25
☐	25179	FIRST, LAST, AND ALWAYS #96 Barbara Conklin	$2.25
☐	25244	DANCING IN THE DARK #97 Carolyn Ross	$2.25
☐	25245	LOVE IS IN THE AIR #98 Diana Gregory	$2.25
☐	25297	ONE BOY TOO MANY #99 Marian Caudell	$2.25
☐	26747	FOLLOW THAT BOY #100 Debra Spector	$2.50
☐	25366	WRONG FOR EACH OTHER #101 Debra Spector	$2.25
☐	25367	HEARTS DON'T LIE #102 Terri Fields	$2.25
☐	25429	CROSS MY HEART #103 Diana Gregory	$2.25
☐	25428	PLAYING FOR KEEPS #104 Janice Stevens	$2.25
☐	25469	THE PERFECT BOY #105 Elizabeth Reynolds	$2.25
☐	25470	MISSION: LOVE #106 Kathryn Maris	$2.25
☐	25535	IF YOU LOVE ME #107 Barbara Steiner	$2.25
☐	25536	ONE OF THE BOYS #108 Jill Jarnow	$2.25
☐	25643	NO MORE BOYS #109 White	$2.25
☐	25642	PLAYING GAMES #110 Eileen Hehl	$2.25
☐	25726	STOLEN KISSES #111 Elizabeth Reynolds	$2.50
☐	25727	LISTEN TO YOUR HEART #112 Marian Caudell	$2.50
☐	25814	PRIVATE EYES #113 Julia Winfield	$2.50
☐	25815	JUST THE WAY YOU ARE #114 Janice Boies	$2.50

Prices and availability subject to change without notice.